by Henry Winkler a

HANK ZIPZER

the world's greatest underachiever

I Got a "D" in Salami

by Henry Winkler and Lin Oliver

HANK ZIPZER

the world's greatest underachiever

I Got a "D" in Salami

Grosset & Dunlap
An Imprint of Penguin Group (USA) Inc.

Cover illustration by Tim Heitz

GROSSET & DUNLAP
Published by the Penguin Group
Penguin Group (USA) Inc., 375 Hudson Street, New York, New York 10014, USA
Penguin Group (Canada), 90 Eglinton Avenue East, Suite 700,
Toronto, Ontario M4P 2Y3, Canada
(a division of Pearson Penguin Canada Inc.)
Penguin Books Ltd, 80 Strand, London WC2R 0RL, England
Penguin Ireland, 25 St Stephen's Green, Dublin 2, Ireland
(a division of Penguin Books Ltd)
Penguin Group (Australia), 707 Collins Street, Melbourne, Victoria 3008, Australia
(a division of Pearson Australia Group Pty Ltd)
Penguin Books India Pvt Ltd, 11 Community Centre,
Panchsheel Park, New Delhi–110 017, India
Penguin Group (NZ), 67 Apollo Drive, Rosedale, Auckland 0632, New Zealand
(a division of Pearson New Zealand Ltd)
Penguin Books (South Africa), Rosebank Office Park, 181 Jan Smuts Avenue,
Parktown North 2193, South Africa
Penguin China, B7 Jiaming Center, 27 East Third Ring Road North,
Chaoyang District, Beijing 100020, China

Penguin Books Ltd, Registered Offices: 80 Strand, London WC2R 0RL, England

Text copyright © 2003 by Henry Winkler and Lin Oliver Productions, Inc. Cover illustration copyright © 2013 by Grosset & Dunlap. Interior illustrations copyright © 2003 by Grosset & Dunlap. All rights reserved. Published by Grosset & Dunlap, a division of Penguin Young Readers Group, 345 Hudson Street, New York, New York, 10014. GROSSET & DUNLAP is a trademark of Penguin Group (USA) Inc. Printed in the U.S.A.

Library of Congress Control Number: 2003004905

ISBN: 978-0-448-43163-5   10 9 8 7 6 5 4 3 2 1

This book is dedicated to Hank's godfather,
Alan Berger, who had the bright idea
to introduce us—HW and LO

CHAPTER 1

"**Hank, will you** please stop bouncing around like a jumping bean and concentrate?" my mom asked.

"This is what I do when I concentrate," I answered.

I was hopping over to a sock that was lying on the floor of my room. When I reached the sock, I picked it up with my toes. That's a trick I learned from one of my best friends, Ashley Wong. Ashley can pick up almost anything with her toes, including marbles. She can also tie a cherry stem into a knot using only her tongue. Those are qualities you want in a best friend.

I curled my toes around the sock until I had it in my grasp. Then I swung my leg around to the side so it was sticking straight out from my body. That's a trick I learned from my other best friend, Frankie Townsend. His mom is a yoga teacher, and she taught him how to twist his legs around like a pretzel. Frankie has gotten so good at it that he can bring his big toe all the way up to his nose, which is also an excellent way to check if your feet smell. I never thought about this before, but my friends and I all have very talented toes. Maybe that's why we're friends.

When my leg was in the right position, I released the sock from my toe grasp and flicked it into the air toward my dirty laundry hamper. It was an excellent flick, if I do say so myself. The sock sailed into the hamper and landed dead center on my boxers.

"He shoots, he scores!" I yelled, doing my wiggly victory dance.

My mom shook her head. "I came in here to help you study your spelling words," she said with a sigh. "But frankly, Hank, I have better things to do with my time than watch you play toe basketball."

We had been studying for a while, and my Mom sounded like she was getting a little crabby. I sat down at my desk chair and got serious.

"Hit me with the next word," I said to her. "I'm ready for it."

"Receive," said my mom. "Think before you answer, Hank. It's a tricky one."

I looked across the room, trying to see the word in my head. But instead, all I saw was my other sock, lying on the floor next to the hamper. I tried not to go for it, but I couldn't resist. I scooted across the room on my chair, doing a three-sixty spin at the halfway point. I don't know who invented chairs with wheels, but whoever the guy was, he was a genius.

"I thought you were going to focus, Hank," my mom said, grabbing onto the back of my chair and bringing me to a screeching stop.

"Believe it or not, I'm trying to."

She didn't like that answer. She shot me one of those Mom looks that says *Don't try to fool me, young man; I see what you're up to.* I'll bet you've probably gotten that look before.

"I'm serious," I tried to explain to her. "I have this theory that if I keep moving, then my brain won't stop and I won't forget my spelling words. I'll bet it works. *Receive* is the word, right?"

She nodded.

"Okay," I said. "Receive. R, right?"

She started to answer, but I put my hand up to stop her. "Don't tell me. Don't tell me. Okay. Receive. R-E-C-I-E-V-E. See? Didn't I tell you it works?"

"Hank, I hate to tell you this, but you reversed two letters."

"Okay, okay. Don't tell me what they are," I said. "Receive. Okay." I took my time and thought really hard as I spelled out the letters. "R-E-C-E-I-V-E."

"That's great," my mom said. "You got it!"

I gave her a high five. It felt good to be right.

"You have just seen my new Hank Zipzer guaranteed method for getting one hundred percent," I said. "I'm going to win the spelling contest tomorrow, Mom. I am Spelling Man, Ruler of the Alphabet."

"Not so fast, Spelling Man," my mom laughed. "There's one more word left on your list."

One word? Piece of cake. I had already learned fourteen. Fourteen words neatly packed away in my brain for tomorrow's contest. It had taken most of the night, but it would be worth it just to see the look on Ms. Adolf's face when I won.

Ms. Adolf, my fourth grade-teacher, was going to be amazed. Hey, I was amazed. Never before in my whole life had I ever known how to spell all—I mean *all*—my words correctly. Spelling is one of the hardest things on the face of the earth for me. I study. I go over and over and over my spelling words. At the time, they seem to stick to my memory. They seem to be happy in my brain. But then later, like the next morning when I really need them, they seem to have orbited off into space somewhere. Or if not space, then wherever lost spelling words go. It's like they slip off the edge of my brain.

But this time I felt different. Tonight I was the master. I was the king of the country of Spelling.

I flung myself onto the bottom bunk of my bed and bounced around. "What's the last word?" I asked my Mom.

"Rhythm," she said.

That was a tough one. I knew it had a lot of letters you couldn't hear, but exactly what they were was a total mystery to me. I flipped myself over and hung off the edge of the bed. All the blood flowed into my head, and I wondered if a person's face could explode from doing that.

"Hank?" I could hear my Mom asking. She sounded like she was far away. It was really loud inside my head, with all that blood beating like a drum. I poked around under my bed. There was a lot of interesting stuff there: a stuffed Tasmanian Devil I had won at my school fair, a plastic golf club, a pencil sharpener in the shape of the Empire State Building, and a dust ball the size of a fist.

Suddenly the dust ball moved, and from behind it, two beady eyes stared out at me. The eyes moved! Then a long, snakelike tongue shot out at me with the speed of a bullet. I flew off the bed like a rocket.

"Emily!" I screamed. "Get your creepy reptile out of here!"

My sister Emily is so weird that she has an iguana for a pet. How many eight-year-old girls do you know who sleep with a large, scaly lizard in their bed at night? Why can't she have a teddy bear like everyone else's little sister?

Emily came racing in. She was wearing my Mets sweatshirt, which she can do because we're about the same size. Even though she's fifteen months younger than I am, she's a little tall for her age and I'm a little short for mine.

"Emily, that's my sweatshirt," I said. "Give it back."

"Why should I?"

"You don't even like baseball," I said. "You're just trying to make me mad."

"Will you stop yelling, Hank," she said. "You're scaring Katherine."

"You got it backwards, backwad," I said. "Katherine scared me."

Emily bent down and coaxed Katherine out from under the bed. "Come on, girl," she said, in her iguana-talking voice. "Come to your mommy lizard." Could she be any weirder?

The dust ball had attached itself to Katherine's face and was hanging off where her lips would be if iguanas had lips. She looked like a scaly Santa Claus with a mutant beard.

"How is a guy supposed to study his spelling words with that lizard hanging out under his bed?" I asked.

"Since when are you studying spelling?" Emily answered, putting Katherine on her shoulder.

"Since tonight," I said. "We're having a spelling contest tomorrow, and Ms. Adolf has promised that the winner gets an A in spelling on his report card. That's going to be me."

"I only see one problem," said Emily. "You can't spell. Remember?"

"Watch and learn," I said with my most confident voice. I turned to my mom. "Rhythm. That's the word, right?"

"That's the one," my mom said.

I opened my mouth to spell the word. I noticed that nothing was coming out. Suddenly, I felt a little nauseous. I knew that the word was there in my mind, but I was worried that if I tried to get it, it would loosen up and float away.

Six eyes stared at me, waiting. My mom's blue ones, encouraging me to give it a try. Emily's green ones, expecting me to get it wrong. Katherine's beady ones, giving up no clue as to what goes on inside an iguana's head. *Here goes nothing*, I thought.

"R-H-Y-T-" I stopped. *Come on, Hank.* I started again.

"R-H-Y-T-H-U-M," I said.

"Wrong," said Emily, as happy as a clam. "It's r-h-y-t-h-m. There's no U—as in U can't spell."

"Maybe I can't spell," I said, "but at least I don't have iguana poop on my shoulder."

Emily looked on her shoulder, and sure enough, Katherine had left a little pool of poop there for Emily to enjoy. I laughed.

"I wouldn't laugh if I were you," she said. "Remember whose sweatshirt this is."

"I'm warning you! You better wash it at least a hundred times." I started for her, lizard and all, but Mom stopped me.

"That's enough, you two," she said. "Emily, take your iguana back to your room. Hank, why don't you and Dad go over the words one more time. I'm taking my bath."

Trust me, if there's one person you don't want to study your spelling words with, it's my dad. He's a crossword-puzzle nut, and he knows how to spell every word in every language and their abbreviations. And on top of that, he can't even begin to understand why spelling is hard for me.

"Just sit your butt down in your chair and study," he says all the time. "If you study, spelling is a can't-lose situation."

So I walked out of my room and sat my butt down on a chair in the living room. My dad was in his favorite chair, watching a TV talk show where a bunch of grown-ups talk all at once. And they say kids have bad manners. His glasses were up on top of his head, which is where he puts them when he's not reading or doing a crossword puzzle. He always forgets they're up there. Lots of times, he walks around, looking for his glasses, and we have to tell him they're on top of his head. He needs glasses to find his glasses.

"Do you want me to quiz you?" my dad asked.

Should I impress him? Should I try one word? No. I decided to just let the words rest up in my head so they would come flying out of my mouth when I needed them in class.

"Thanks, Dad," I answered, "but I've studied enough. I think I'll just get a good night's sleep."

I kissed him goodnight. I always kiss him on the left cheek. It's dangerous to kiss him on the right one—you could get poked with a pencil. My dad keeps a pencil tucked behind his right ear. He keeps it there in case he suddenly remembers a word he's been trying to think of. If you're as much of a crossword-puzzle maniac as my dad is, you don't want to let something as important as a four-letter word for nostril get away from you.

I went in the bathroom to get ready for bed. As I brushed my teeth, I let myself imagine what it would feel like to win the spelling contest. Ms. Adolf would smile at me for the first time ever. I closed my eyes and I saw her handing me an A. Not a paper one either, but a solid gold one, like the statues movie stars get at the Oscars. My gold A would be so heavy that I'd have trouble carrying it back to my seat. I'd put it up on my desk so that everyone in my class or passing by our door could see it. Every kid in the class would congratulate me, even the class bully, Nick "The Tick" McKelty. Oh yeah, he'd smile at me with his big snaggly teeth and say, "I wish that was mine." That would be sweet.

I opened my eyes, looked into the mirror, and imagined my classmates slapping me on the back. I smiled. My teeth were blue from my gel toothpaste.

"Thank you very much. Yes, I am very proud of myself. Very, very proud."

As I said the word "proud," a big wad of toothpaste flew out of my mouth and splattered all over the bathroom mirror. I started to wipe it off with my Mets washcloth. I looked around to see if anyone was watching and then scooped a little of the gel onto my finger. I used it to write on the mirror.

"R-h-y-t-h-m," I wrote in sparkly blue letters. I stepped back and stared at the word. For once, it was spelled correctly. I did my wiggly victory dance.

I could hardly wait for the next day. I was going to get my first A.

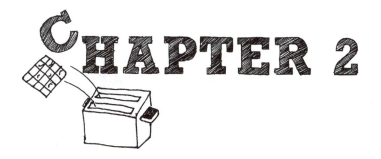

CHAPTER 2

I must have slept through my alarm, because the next morning I woke up ten minutes later than usual. The last thing I wanted was to be late for school—or "tardy," as Ms. Adolf says. Ms. Adolf told us that tardy pupils don't get to participate in spelling contests. If you're even thirty seconds late to class, she writes a big, red *T* next to your name in her roll book. She once sent Ryan Shimozato to Principal Love's office for having two *T*'s in a row, even though he had a sprained ankle from soccer and had to walk with crutches. I don't know if Ms. Adolf is the meanest fourth grade teacher that ever lived, but she's in the top three for sure.

I threw on some clothes, grabbed a waffle from the toaster, and flew out the door and into the elevator. I wished I had the time to soak the waffle in syrup, but I knew Ashley and Frankie were already waiting for me in front of our building. Frankie lives on the sixth floor and Ashley lives on the fourth. It's so great to have your best friends live in the same building. We don't have to schedule play dates like lots of other kids in our class. Whenever we want to get together, we just pick up the phone and say, "Meet me in the basement." That's where we have our clubhouse, which is also the World Headquarters for Magik 3, our magic act.

Frankie is an amazing magician. Ashley and I are his assistants. Magik 3 has performed in public two times. The first time, at my grandpa's bowling league party, we were a smash hit. The second time was at Tyler King's fourth birthday party. His family lives across the hall from me. His mom had heard how good we were at the bowling party and she offered us fifteen dollars to do a magic show at Tyler's party. For our opening, Frankie said his special magic word, which is "Zengawii," and made a quarter appear out of Tyler's ear. The problem was Tyler said he wanted a million more quarters. When Frankie tried to explain that he didn't have a million quarters, Tyler went bonkers and said he hated the Zengawii man and wanted him to go back to his magic castle and never come back. He's still saying that to everyone he sees, so we're waiting until he calms down before we hand out our business cards in the building.

Frankie and Ashley were outside, hopping up and down to keep their feet warm. I shivered when I hit the cold air. It was the first week in November, and I could feel the New York winter just around the corner.

Unlike myself, Frankie and Ashley were dressed for the weather. Ashley was wearing a purple parka with a matching purple hat that she had decorated with rhinestones. She glues rhinestones onto all her clothes—even her tennis shoes and the frames of her glasses. That's Ashley for you. Frankie had on a Yankees jacket.

"Did you have to wear that?" I asked him, like the loyal Mets fan that I am.

"Yes, I did, Zip," he said, "because I dress like a winner."

"Fine, then I'll let you borrow my Mets sweatshirt."

"The Mets? Those losers?"

"Our day will come," I shot back. "Mets fans are patient."

"You two have to stop this right now or we'll never get to school," said Ashley, who isn't a baseball fan at all. Believe it or not, she watches professional Ping-Pong.

I don't know how much you know about baseball, so let me just tell you this right now. If you live in New York and like baseball, you're either a Mets fan or a Yankees fan. You can't be both. Mets fans like the underdog, the team that comes from behind. Yankees fans go for the easy win. But that's just my opinion. It says a lot about my friendship with Frankie that we can be such good friends even though we're on different sides of the fence, baseball-wise.

"Hank, you're going to be cold," said Frankie's father, Dr. Townsend, who was walking us to school. Dr. Townsend isn't the kind of doctor you go to when you have a sore throat. He's a doctor of African-American studies, which is what he teaches at Columbia University. "Where's your jacket?"

"Oops," I said. "I'll be right back."

My father always says, "What you don't

have in your mind you have in your feet," meaning I had to go all the way back upstairs to get my jacket. There was no time to wait for the elevator, so I ran up the ten flights to our apartment. I dashed inside and grabbed for my jacket, but it wasn't in the closet where I had left it—or at least, where I thought I had left it.

"Mom, have you seen my green jacket?" I hollered. I was breathing hard from the run upstairs.

My dad came out of the bedroom in his T-shirt and boxer shorts, which is not really something you want to see first thing in the morning. Actually, it's not something you want to see any time of the day.

"Your mother already left," he said. "She had to take Emily to a dental appointment."

Now, ordinarily, I would've asked something like, "Why, were her fangs bothering her?" But Frankie is always telling me about good karma. He got that from his mom, who is big believer in karma. Basically, karma means that if you put out something good, you get something good back. If you put out something rotten, it comes back and bites you in the tush.

Since I really, really wanted to win the spelling contest, I figured this was no day to take any chances with my karma, so I decided to hold off on the fangs remark.

Instead, I said to my dad, "Poor Emily. I sure hope the dentist doesn't do anything that's going to hurt her." Boy, if that didn't guarantee me some excellent karma, I don't know what would.

My dad was looking around for my jacket, grumbling about how I never put anything where it belongs.

"There it is," I said, pointing to our dachshund, Cheerio. Cheerio was lying on the couch, looking so cute all curled up on my jacket. I gently pulled it out from under him.

"Don't go nuts on me, boy" I whispered. "I'm in a hurry."

Cheerio went nuts anyway. He jumped off the couch and started to spin around in a circle. When he does that, which is pretty often, he looks like a big, furry cheerio, which is how he got his name. Our vet says his spinning thing is a reaction to stress. I don't know what he's got to be stressed about. I mean, all he has to do is eat and pee. No one's asking him to spell *receive* or *rhythm*.

I put on my jacket and ran downstairs. Frankie was looking at his watch.

"We thought maybe you went upstairs and went back to bed, didn't we Ashweena?" he said. Frankie has nicknames for everyone. He calls his dad "Double T," because his name is Thomas Townsend.

"We better get a move on. We don't want to be tardy, do we?" Ashley asked, doing a pretty good imitation of Ms. Adolf.

It's two blocks from our building to our school. We had to walk really fast to get to there on time. Luckily, we arrived just before the bell rang. We said good-bye to Dr. Townsend, raced upstairs, and slid into our seats just as Ms. Adolf was closing our classroom door.

Ms. Adolf was wearing a gray skirt and blouse, just like she had worn the day before and the day before that and every day since school started. I guess she figures gray looks good on her because it matches her gray face. You should see her hairdo. It looks like she has a stack of hairy gray doughnuts piled up on top of her head. I'm sorry if this grosses you out, but I have to tell it like I see it.

The other teachers on our floor still had their Halloween decorations up, but not our class. In fact, Ms. Adolf had never put any up in the first place. She thinks Halloween is a silly holiday, because all you do is dress up and eat candy and have fun. I bet her favorite holiday to celebrate is the Day of the Dead.

Instead of ghosts and goblins and pumpkins, the walls of our class are decorated with artwork from our states project. We each picked a state and outlined it in the color of the product it was most famous for. For example, Florida is orange because of its orange groves, and Vermont is brown because of its maple syrup. I had picked Rhode Island because I like the shape of it. I outlined it in red for the red hen, which is the state bird. Rhode Island is the smallest state, and its motto is "Hope." If people had mottos, I think I'd pick "Hope" for mine. I sure do hope a lot. In fact, I was hoping that I would win the spelling contest that morning.

"Now, pupils, today is our spelling contest,"

Ms. Adolf said, "and we're all going to have great fun. I know I am."

Call me crazy, but I don't know how anyone can think spelling is even *slightly* fun, let alone *great* fun. Roller coasters are fun. Riding bikes in the park is fun. Baseball games are fun. But spelling is definitely not fun, unless you're the type of person who enjoys getting shots at the doctor. Then you'd probably think spelling is a barrel of laughs.

"Here are the rules," said Ms. Adolf. "Pupils will be asked to spell fifteen words, the ones I assigned to each of you at the beginning of the week. Those pupils who get all the words on their list correct may participate in the final round, which covers all the words on all lists. As soon as you miss a word in this round, you must sit down. The last pupil standing will be the winner and will receive an A on his or her report card. Are there any questions?"

Luke Whitman put his hand up.

"Can I go to the nurse's office and lie down?" he asked. "I feel sick." Luke Whitman asks if he can go to the nurse's office every single day, and Ms. Adolf's answer is always the same.

"Absolutely not," said Ms. Adolf. "Now, who wants to go first in today's spelling contest?"

Nick McKelty put his thick arm in the air and waved it around like he had a gigantic bathroom emergency.

"I'll go first!" he grunted. "I am totally, two hundred percent prepared."

He always says things like that. He claims his parents are best friends with the mayor of New York, or he tells you he got the highest math score ever recorded in the western hemisphere. We call it The McKelty Factor—truth times a hundred.

Even though Nick the Tick was acting like a total jerk, secretly I was glad he put his hand up. At least it meant that Ms. Adolf wasn't going to call on me. Usually she calls on me first. I think it makes her happy when I don't have the right answer, no matter what the subject.

As McKelty got up to go to the front of the classroom, he walked close enough to me that I got a mega-whiff of his bad, bad breath. He must have eaten an entire raw onion for breakfast, because his breath smelled like a rhinoceros with tooth decay. Not that I know what a rhinoceros with tooth decay smells like, but I'll bet it's pretty foul.

"Hey, girls," McKelty said to Frankie and me as he walked by. "Ready to see a spelling master at work?"

"Sure, Nick," Frankie whispered. "Who you got in mind?"

I laughed, and Ms. Adolf shot me a wicked look.

"Since you seem to find this so funny, Henry, you'll go next," she said.

I wish she'd call me Hank. No one calls me Henry, except my mom when she's really mad, and Paula, the woman who makes appointments at my dentist's office. No one but Ms. Adolf, that is. I've told her a million times that all my friends call me Hank. She says she sees no need for that, because my real name is Henry. Besides, she's not my friend.

My heart started to beat faster. I looked over at Frankie, who gave me his famous smile we call The Big Dimple. He says a lot with that smile. This time, it said, *You can do it, Zip. Just breathe.*

Frankie must tell me to breathe four times a day. As a matter of fact, he tells everyone to breathe if he thinks they are getting too tense about things.

Ms. Adolf gave Nick fifteen words to spell. As usual, he was all talk and no walk. Out of the fifteen words, he spelled seven right and missed eight. No A for him, that millipede.

All during his turn, I tried to review my words. My brain was swimming in letters. They were all over the place but not making themselves into any words I knew. *Breathe*, I said to myself. *You can do this, Hank. Piece of cake.* I tried really hard to talk myself into believing my own words. But in my brain, right underneath those words, were the other more familiar words: *No way, Hank.*

CHAPTER 3

Ms. Adolf must have called my name, but I was concentrating so hard, I didn't hear her at first. All of a sudden, I saw her standing over me. The entire class was staring at me. Every eye was burning into my skin.

"Daydreaming, are we?" Ms. Adolf asked.

"No," I answered. "Just practicing my words. I guess I can't spell and hear at the same time."

The kids cracked up, and I had to smile. There it was, the old Zipzer attitude. I still had it. I didn't mean to be funny, but the sound of the kids enjoying my answer did feel good.

The feeling didn't last, however.

"Come with me, young man," Ms. Adolf commanded. I walked up to the front of the room and turned toward the class.

As I looked out at all the faces, my ears

stopped working for real. It was as if everything was moving in slow motion. I looked over at Ms. Adolf and saw her lips move, but I couldn't hear a thing.

Ms. Adolf repeated the word "rhythm." I read her lips. *Come on Hank, breathe. You know this word.*

My body started working again.

"Rhythm," I said. "R-H-Y-T-H-M, rhythm." Without realizing it, I high-fived myself. The class laughed again.

"Quiet! This is not a laughing matter," Ms. Adolph reminded them. "All right, Mr. Comedian. Try 'receive'."

"R-E-C . . ." I paused. So far, so good. Then my mind went totally blank.

R-E-C-what? I know there's an E and an I, but which comes first? What's the rule? I before E except after—Oh no, what's the word? I forgot the word. What word was I spelling? How can I be so stupid? Breathe . . . I am breathing. I'm just not remembering.

"Well, Henry, there is more to the word receive than R-E-C," Ms. Adolf said.

Oh, yeah, thank goodness—receive!

"I know this; don't tell me," I blurted out with confidence.

"Oh, trust me, I won't," Ms. Adolf assured me.

"R-E-C-I-E-V-E, receive." *Oh please, oh please, let that be right.*

"I thought you said you knew it," she said. "I'll give you one more chance. Try 'neighbor.'"

"Neighbor," I said. "N-A . . ." *Where did it go?*

Last night I knew every one of these words forward and backward. This morning, I'd lost them. From the time I left my apartment until the time I arrived in class, they must've fallen out of my head. Maybe I lost them on the street or in the hallway or the stairwell coming up to the classroom.

I started to hit my forehead. Maybe I could shake them loose from their hiding place in my brain. *How can this be happening?*

"What are you doing, Henry?" asked Ms. Adolf.

"I'm trying to wake my brain up. Maybe the words are holding onto the sides of my brain and won't fall down into my mouth." The class laughed again, but this time I really wasn't being funny.

"Try 'separate,'" Ms. Adolf said.

"Do I have to?"

"Try 'separate' now."

"I know it starts with an S."

"Sit down, Henry."

"But, Ms. Adolf, I studied these words. I know this."

"I'm going to count to three, Henry. If you're not in your seat when I say three, you're going to Principal Love's office."

"Ms. Adolf, you believe in second chances, don't you? Sure you do." I was begging.

"One . . ."

"Just give me another minute. It takes a while for my brain to fire up. I'm like an old car—I just have to give it a little gas."

"Two. . . ."

"Please don't say three, Ms. Adolf. Just let me try one more word, because I'm feeling like I can. . . ."

"Three."

She said it. She said three.

I can't believe she said three.

CHAPTER 4

As I walked down the stairs to Principal Love's office, I felt like I had taken that walk a hundred times before. I felt that way because I had.

Principal Love and I have spent a whole lot of time together, having long talks. And I don't mean the "How about those Mets?" kind of talks, either. Nope, the kind of talks I have with Principal Love is listening to him tell me what I've done wrong, and according to him, that's pretty much everything.

I don't know how this happens. I try to behave in school. I'm not like Nick McKelty, who gets a kick out of being a jerk. And I'm certainly not like Luke Whitman, whose full-time job is getting into trouble. I try to follow the rules. I try hard, but somehow I always wind up doing face time with Principal Love.

For example, take the first day of fourth grade. Ms. Adolf said we had to write a five-paragraph essay describing what we did during summer vacation. It's really hard for me to write a five-paragraph essay, so I decided to create a living essay. Instead of writing about our visit to Niagara Falls, I made a model of Niagara Falls out of papier-mâché. I even hooked it up to the sink in our class so that real water could run through it. Was it my fault that the water overflowed and gushed all over the floor? Was it my fault that Ms. Adolf got blasted in the face by the water hose? Was it my fault that Principal Love stepped on a floating lunch bag and a tuna sandwich exploded in his face?

I reached the first floor and walked toward the office. Mrs. Crock was in the attendance office, and looked up when she saw me.

"Oh, no, Hank." She sighed. "Not again."

"Mrs. Crock," I said. "Would you like to hear me spell 'separate'?"

"Why, yes, dear, if you'd like to," she answered.

"S-E-P-A-R-A-T-E," I said.

"That's very lovely spelling, dear," she said.

"Have a seat on the bench, and I'll page Principal Love. He's in the cafeteria."

I sat down on the bench in the hall. Separate. There it was, just waiting on the tip of my tongue. I knew it was there all along. If only Ms. Adolf had given me another chance.

I heard footsteps approaching, but I knew it wasn't Principal Love. He always wears rubber-soled Velcro shoes that make a squeaking sound on the linoleum when he walks. These footsteps were clicking, not squeaking.

"Hank? Is that you?" a man's voice asked.

I looked up. It was Mr. Rock. Mr. Rock is the music teacher at PS 87. I met him at the beginning of the school year, when I did a week of detention in his classroom after school. We did the coolest things, like listen to music and talk about our all-time favorite cars. I was so embarrassed that he was seeing me in the principal's office.

"Ms. Adolf sent me to see Principal Love," I told him, before he could ask.

"What's your crime?" He asked it like he was joking around.

"I wouldn't sit down during the spelling contest."

"Forty lashes with a wet noodle for you."

He smiled. He was joking around! Mr. Rock is the nicest teacher you could ever hope to meet.

Squeak, squeak, squeak. Principal Love and his dancing Velcro feet were coming down the hall. I stood up and got nervous. Mr. Rock leaned over and whispered in my ear.

"Speak up for yourself in there, Hank," he said. "You're a great kid."

Then he gave me a high five and left.

When he saw me at his office door, Principal Love did not look happy. Neither did his mole.

Principal Love has this mole on his face that I swear looks like the Statue of Liberty without the torch. Ashley and Frankie disagree. Ashley thinks it looks like a cherry pit. Frankie says it looks like one of those crackers that's shaped like a goldfish. But I say my opinion goes, since I've spent way more time in Principal Love's office than both Frankie and Ashley combined. I've had a lot of mole-viewing time.

"I see we meet again, Mr. Zipzer," Principal Love said in his big-man voice. Even though he's not much taller than I am, Principal Love has a really loud voice. He always sounds like he's on the loudspeaker system, even though he isn't.

I followed him into his office.

"Sit down, young man," he said, pointing to the chair across from his desk. "You're spending so much time here, I believe that seat is starting to take the shape of your rear end."

I laughed. He didn't.

"I'll let you know when something funny happens," he said. "Until then, keep your laughter to yourself."

He read over the note Ms. Adolf sent with me, rubbing his chin as he read. He was dangerously close to touching his mole. I wonder if when he touches it, he screams, "Ick!" I know I would.

"I read here that Ms. Adolf asked you to sit down and you did not," he said.

I cleared my throat and tried to speak. Something came out, but it wasn't words. It was mostly air, with a croaking froggy sound mixed in. Principal Love makes you nervous, even if you're trying not to be nervous.

"Speak up, young man," he said.

I tried again, and a few words came out this time. "I wasn't finished spelling, sir."

"But your directions were to sit down," he said. "Were they not?"

I didn't answer, but everyone at PS 87 knows that when Leland Love asks a question, he likes to answer it himself.

"Yes, they were," he said, proving my point.

"I'm going to tell you something, Mr. Zipzer," he said, "and I want you to carry this thought with you for the rest of your school years. It may be the best single piece of advice you ever get."

Wow. I was ready for that. I scooted up on the edge of my chair. *Lay it on me*, I thought.

Principal Love cleared his throat.

"Following directions will get you where you need to be, no matter where you are," he said.

If that is the best piece of advice I'll ever get, I hope I never hear the worst.

"It just so happens that you have caught me in a very good mood," said Principal Love, "and so I'm going to let you off with a warning." He reached down and loosened one of the Velcro straps on his shoes. "Do you know why I'm in a good mood, Mr. Zipzer?"

"Because you really, really love your Velcro shoes?" I asked.

"That's one reason," he said. "They are so convenient. But the second reason is that today is fish day in the cafeteria, and I am about to go and enjoy a fine piece of halibut. Just for the halibut, that is."

He threw his head back and laughed so loud it gave me the creeps. "Something funny just happened," he said. "You may laugh now, Mr. Zipzer."

He laughed again, and the Statue of Liberty mole wiggled back and forth as if it was doing the hula. *It must like fish, too*, I thought.

CHAPTER 5

The only decent thing about the spelling contest was that Ashley won. She is such a good friend that her winning almost made up for the fact that my spelling was a total disaster.

"Cheer up, Zip," Frankie said to me, as we sat down at our table in the lunchroom. "So, you're not a speller. Big deal."

"I'm also not an adder or a subtracter or a reader or a writer," I said. "Let's face it, Frankie. I'm a school flop."

I was feeling pretty terrible. First, I messed up the spelling contest, for no good reason that I could understand. Then I got sent to the principal's office. And if those things hadn't made the day horrible enough, the halibut made the entire lunchroom smell like toxic waste.

"There's more to life than school," said Frankie, pulling out his peanut-butter-and-jelly sandwich. "Don't get down on yourself."

That's easy for Frankie to say. He's one of those kids who's good at everything. He reads like a grown-up—even the newspaper. He actually *reads* the sports section every day. Not me. I have to watch ESPN for my updates. He's also totally funny, a phenomenal magician, and all the girls like him, too.

"What's up, Frankie?" asked Katie Sperling and Kim Paulson as they walked by with their trays.

See what I mean? The two most beautiful girls in the fourth grade weren't asking, "What's up, Hank?"

My father always says that Frankie Townsend is going to be the next African-American president of the United States. Of course, he also says that Emily is going to be a rocket scientist, as though that's ever going to happen. I can see it now: Emily cruising around Mission Control with Katherine—flashing her sticky tongue at all the astronauts—on her shoulder. *Houston, we have a problem. We have an ugly iguana loose on the launchpad with its tongue stuck to the windshield.*

I pulled out my sandwich. My mom had packed me another one of her science experiments. Inside the Baggie with my sandwich was a note from her.

Hi honey,
This is soy-salami-pimento loaf.
Tell me what you think.
Love, Mom

My mom runs a deli called The Crunchy Pickle, which my grandfather Papa Pete started. When she took over the deli, my mom said she wanted to bring lunch meats into the world of healthy eating. So she's always inventing stuff like soy-salami-pimento loaf. I'm her number-one guinea pig.

"That stuff looks nasty," Frankie said, giving my sandwich the evil eye. "Here, buddy. Have half of mine. Yours looks like it has a rash, with all those red spots."

The peanut-butter-and-jelly tasted great. It was the first good thing that had happened to me that day.

Ashley arrived with her tray. Her parents are

both doctors. They don't usually have time to make her lunch in the mornings.

"Robert alert," she said, shaking her chocolate milk. "Sorry, guys. I couldn't ditch him. He's on me like glue."

Robert Upchurch was following Ashley to our table. He lives in our building, and even though he's only in the third grade, he thinks he's best friends with us. We don't have the heart to tell him he's not. I mean, the kid wears a tie to school every day. He's already got a hard enough life, right?

Robert took a seat next to me.

"Greetings," he said, which is a typical Robert thing to say. He talks like he's an alien in a movie. They're always saying stuff like, "I bring you greetings from my people."

A horrible smell drifted up into my nose. It was coming from Robert's tray. I couldn't believe it. He actually got the halibut—school cafeteria fish, the lowest of the low.

"Robert, I can't believe you got the fish," I said. "I've never seen anyone get the fish."

"Actually, fish is excellent for the brain," Robert said. "It's full of fatty oils that provide nutrients that the brain needs to function. Maybe that's why I'm so intelligent."

"Or maybe that's why you smell so bad," said Frankie, holding his nose.

Robert laughed. You have to give him credit for that. You can say almost anything to him and he doesn't take offense.

"How was the spelling contest?" he asked, chomping down on a mouthful of fish.

"Can we talk about something else?" I asked.

"Sure," said Robert. "Would you like to talk penguins? I know a great deal about the King penguin. Actually, it weighs up to forty pounds and grows to be three feet tall."

Without taking a breath, Robert launched into the life cycle of the penguin. It was like having a National Geographic special right there at your lunch table.

Suddenly, I smelled something really foul behind me. Immediately, I realized it was the unmistakable odor of a rhinoceros with tooth decay—Nick McKelty breath.

"Nice work today on the spelling, dodo brain," McKelty said, leaning over my shoulder to grab the last of my sandwich.

"You didn't exactly light up the room your-self, McKelty," I said.

"I just didn't want to make you stupid ones feel bad," McKelty said. "I knew every word."

"Right," said Frankie. "And my name is Bernice."

From the next table, Katie and Kim cracked up. Everyone loves it when Frankie does his "Bernice" line. Everyone but McKelty, that is. Bullies don't like to be laughed at. He pulled himself up to his full height, and I have to admit, he towered over Frankie.

"Listen, Townsend, you say that one more time, and I'm going have my father call your father," he said. Nick's father owns McKelty's Roll 'N Bowl, the bowling alley where my grandpa plays.

"And what's he going to say?" I asked. "Lane number three is available?"

Now Ryan Shimozato and his crew started to laugh. Luke Whitman cracked up, too, but not too loudly.

"Bowling shoes make your feet stink," Luke said. That's typical Luke Whitman. Luke is one of those kids who'll say disgusting things like "booger slime" or "toe jam" or "diaper doo-doo" for no reason at all. I'll bet there's a kid like that in your class.

McKelty was really mad now. He was searching for a comeback, but the big lug just couldn't come up with anything.

"Frankie," said Ashley, "can you make Mr. McKelty here disappear?"

"No problemo," said Frankie.

He stood up and looked over at Kim and Katie. He flashed them The Big Dimple. Boy, were they going for it, too. But this is what is so cool about Frankie Townsend. He could've done the magic all by himself and gotten all that attention from Katie and Kim for himself. But did he? No. Here's what he did. He took me by the arm and pulled me to my feet.

"I can't do magic without my man here. Zip, give me some of your magical moves, buddy."

Kim and Katie stared at me. In fact, everyone in the cafeteria stopped what they were doing and looked at me. Frankie gave me the nod, and I started to wave my hands around like I was casting a spell. Frankie and I have watched *Behind the Scenes Secrets of Magic* videos until the tapes were practically worn out, so I have the moves down pretty smoothly. I gave it the full show-business treatment. Frankie let me go on until he saw that Katie and Kim were impressed. Then he stood up and closed his eyes. When he spoke, it was almost a whisper.

Bones of halibut, magic thing,
Sound the bell! Zengawii! Ring!

He opened his eyes, and the very second he did, the bell rang. I'm not kidding. It was amazing.

"Lunch is over; everyone back to class," said Mrs. Tomasini, the teacher on lunch duty. "Nick McKelty, that means you. Get going right now. Hustle."

Nick picked up his backpack and hurried out of the cafeteria.

"Wow," Katie said to Frankie. "You did make him disappear."

"You guys are great!" said Kim, smiling at me. "Can I walk back to class with you?"

"Why not," I answered, giving her my big smile. I may be dumb in spelling, but hey, I'm no dummy.

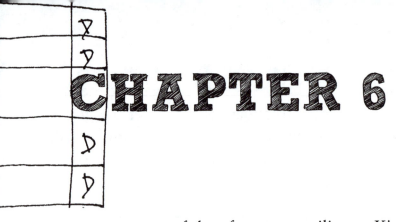

CHAPTER 6

I spent most of the afternoon smiling at Kim Paulson. She sits in front of me, so I was actually smiling at the back of her head. But, trust me, the back of her head is very nice. I couldn't believe how a day that had started out so terribly had turned so good.

I was such a fine mood that it didn't even bother me that much when Ms. Adolf said she was handing out our report cards. It was just before the end of school that day. As we packed up our books, Ms. Adolf went to her desk and unlocked the top drawer with a silver key that she wears around her neck. She took out her roll book, which was stuffed full of envelopes. Then she walked up and down the aisles, handing out the report cards individually. She gave each person a small, white envelope that was addressed to their parents.

When Ms. Adolf arrived at my desk, I put my hand out to receive my white report-card envelope. But instead of handing me one of the small envelopes that everyone else got, Ms. Adolf pulled out a large, brown manila envelope.

"Your report card is inside, Henry, along with a letter to your parents. Please see that they call me immediately."

Everyone sitting around me got quiet. I looked around the class. No one else had gotten a big brown envelope. I didn't know what it meant, but I knew way down in my stomach that it wasn't good. It took exactly one second for Nick McKelty to open his big mouth.

"Dear Mr. and Mrs. Zipzer," he said, making his voice sound like Ms. Adolf. "This is to inform you that your son is a stupid retardo."

A few kids laughed. I was so embarrassed that I could feel the tips of my ears turning red. I grabbed my backpack. I had to get out of there. Fortunately, the bell rang.

"I have to go to the bathroom," I said to Frankie. "I'll meet you downstairs."

I ran to the bathroom, ducked into one of the stalls, and locked the door. I think my hands were shaking as I ripped open the brown envelope. I pulled out my report card and looked at it.

I got a *D* in spelling. But that wasn't the worst of it.

I also got a *D* in reading.

I also got a *D* in math.

There was a note to my parents from Ms. Adolf. It was written in cursive. I couldn't make out all the words, but I got a few of them. *Doesn't follow directions . . . Poor study habits . . . Sloppy work . . . Fails to pay attention . . . Below-average performance.*

It wasn't all bad news, though. I did get a *B*-plus in PE. And let's not forget music. I got a *B*-plus in music, too.

I leaned my head against the door of the stall. I felt like I wanted to throw up.

Look on the bright side, Hank. Make yourself smile. So you'll never learn to read or write or do math. But you're a whiz at dodgeball, and you can carry a tune. Good. When you grow up, you can be a singing dodgeball player.

I tried to laugh at my own joke, but you know what? I cried instead.

CHAPTER 7

I couldn't stay in the bathroom stall forever. I wanted to, but I knew at some point I would have to leave. As I walked downstairs to meet my friends, I made a list in my head.

THE TOP TEN THINGS THAT WILL HAPPEN BECAUSE OF MY REPORT CARD (EXCEPT THERE'S ONLY SEVEN BECAUSE THAT'S ALL I COULD COME UP WITH) BY HANK ZIPZER

1. My parents won't be able to think of a punishment big enough for me. They'll have to hire an evil punishment expert like Darth Vader to think of one.

2. My sister and her iguana will laugh at me for months. And I won't be able to stop them.

3. I will have to repeat the fourth grade forever. Ms. Adolf and I will grow old together, and I'll turn all gray and rinkled like her.

4. My middle name will be changed from Daniel to "Detention King."

6. Kim Paulson will never let me walk to class with her again. I don't even want to walk with me—so why would she?

7. Here's the worst: Nick McKelty will tease me about being stupid, and he'll be right.

8.

CHAPTER 8

Did you notice that I skipped number five on the list?

And that I left off the W in 'wrinkled'?

It's just more proof that I deserve those lousy grades I got.

CHAPTER 9

Frankie and Ashley were waiting for me at the bottom of the stairs. They looked worried.

"Zip, are you okay?" Frankie asked. "You're not looking too good, buddy."

"I'm not feeling too good, either," I said.

"Maybe you have a temperature," Ashley said, putting her hand on my forehead, the way my mom does when she thinks I have a fever.

"Don't touch me in public, Ash," I said. "I'm not that kind of sick anyway. I got bad grades on my report card."

"Like C's?" Ashley asked.

"Ashweena, a C isn't a bad grade," Frankie said. "At least, I don't think it is. Otis got one once in the fourth grade."

Otis is Frankie's older brother. He's in the eighth grade and is smart like Frankie.

"Did he get in trouble?" Ashley asked.

"Not really," Frankie said. "My dad told him a C was a warning sign that he had to work harder. 'Give it some more gas,' he said."

At our school, PS 87, we don't get letter grades until the fourth grade. Up until then, your teachers only write comments on your report card, and they're usually pretty nice. In first grade, my teacher, Ms. Yukelson, wrote, "Hank has excellent scissors skills and has made many valuable contributions to our unit on the harbor." My parents took me out to dinner to celebrate that report card. In third grade, my teacher, Mr. Chan, wrote, "Hank is a natural leader and is well liked by his peers. He needs additional practice in his reading and math skills." We didn't go out and celebrate for that one, but it wasn't terrible, either.

"Not to worry, Zip," Frankie said, throwing his arm around my shoulder. "So what if you got a C or two on your report card? You just got to give it a little more gas, right?"

"Pedal to the metal," said Ashley.

I had to tell them the truth. They were my best friends.

"Listen up, guys. I didn't get a C," I said.

"I got three *D*'s. In spelling, in math, and in reading. And a really bad letter to my parents."

For a minute, Frankie and Ashley didn't say anything. Then Ashley gave me a hug and said I would do better on the next report card. Frankie offered to tutor me in math. I tell you, I have world-class friends.

Robert came to meet us for the walk home. While he was taking off his clip-on tie, which he does every day at exactly ten minutes after three, I told him the news about my report card. There's no point trying to keep anything from Robert. He finds everything out sooner or later. He's like an information magnet.

"I imagine three *D*'s is well below the national average for fourth-graders," Robert said.

"Not now, Robert," Ashley said firmly.

He looked at me like my favorite pet goldfish had just died. Then he did a really weird thing. He asked if he could have my Rollerblades.

"Your parents are going to ground you for so long," he said, "that by the time you get ungrounded, the Rollerblades won't even fit you anymore."

"Not now, Robert," Frankie said, in the same tone Ashley used.

I think, in his own way, Robert was trying to joke around to make me feel better. But all his joke did was bring our attention to that word: *parents*.

My parents weren't going to be happy. It's not that they're mega-strict or anything. It's just that they have expectations. And their main expectation is that my sister and I do well in school. Emily more than meets their expectations—no problem. It's me who's the dud.

I decided that the best thing to do was talk to Papa Pete, who picks us up from school three days a week. Of everyone I know, he'd be the best person to help me figure out a way to break the bad news to my parents.

Papa Pete always seems to understand me when other people don't. I told him that once, when we were sitting on my balcony and sharing a pickle, which is our favorite thing to do. He put his big, hairy arm around me and said, "Hank, my boy. That's what grandpas are for."

He is a great grandpa; there's no doubt about it. But I think it's more than that, too. Papa

Pete says that everyone has a special gift in life. I think I know what his is. He's one of those people who can make you feel good no matter what. For example, one time, when I was little, I stepped on a bee at the beach. It hurt so much that even after the bee sting healed, I limped around for the rest of our vacation. Everyone else in my family teased me about limping so much, but not Papa Pete. He said to me, "Hank, my boy. If I had stepped on that bee, I'd be dragging my whole leg around like a sack of potatoes." Papa Pete never makes you feel bad for what you're feeling, even if what you're feeling is silly.

We walked outside and sat on the steps, waiting for Papa Pete to show up. He was a little late, which wasn't like him. I didn't mind waiting, though. The cold air felt good.

I looked down Amsterdam Avenue. People were crowding along the street, carrying their groceries home, buying a take-out pizza, pushing strollers, walking their kids home from school. They all seemed so happy. I wondered if any of them had ever gotten three *D*'s. That sure can suck the happiness right out of you.

"Hey, look," said Frankie. "It's Silent Stan, the crossword-puzzle man."

I looked across the street, and sure enough, my father was coming toward us.

Uh-oh, I thought, which is not what you want to be thinking when you see your father. *Maybe he has already heard about my report card.*

"Hi, Dad," I said when he reached us. "I thought Papa Pete was coming."

"He's busy," my dad answered. "He called me at home and asked me to get you kids. He's going to meet us at the deli."

He probably has a hot bowling game he can't leave, I thought. Papa Pete spends a lot of time at McKelty's Roll 'N Bowl, where he's the best senior bowler in the league. His team is called The Chopped Livers.

"Hi, kids," my father said, nodding to Frankie and Ashley. "Always good to see you, Robert."

My father really likes Robert, because Robert helps him out with his crossword puzzles. The day before, when my dad couldn't think of a three-letter word for "infection result," Robert came up with "pus." Those moments have given them a special connection.

I should explain that my dad doesn't just lie around the house all day doing crossword puzzles and waiting for calls from Papa Pete. He works at home, doing something with computers. He's tried to describe to me exactly what he does, but when he talks about computer programming, it sounds to me like he's saying, "blah, blah, blahdity, blahdity, blah, blah." I'm not exaggerating, either. My mind just doesn't follow what he's saying.

We started down Amsterdam Avenue, walking fast to keep up with all the people on the street. You have to do that in New York. They don't like slowpokes here.

"So, Mr. Z," Frankie said. "Is Papa Pete okay?"

"He's fine," said my dad. "He had a garlic emergency."

We stopped at the corner of 78th Street and waited for the light to change. My father went on talking, which was strange, because he doesn't usually say much. We leaned in closer so we could hear him over the honking. Two taxis were having a horn-blowing war.

"Vince Gristediano, who owns the biggest supermarket chain in the city, called your mother today," my dad said. "He heard about her vegetarian lunch meats, and he may want to carry her whole line of soy salami in his stores. He asked her to make samples so he can try them out on his store managers tomorrow."

"My mom shops at Gristediano's," said Ashley.

"Actually, everyone does," said Robert. "They have thirty nine markets in Manhattan alone."

"So if Mr. Gristediano buys Mom's soy salamis, will we be rich?" I asked.

"I don't know about that," said my dad. "But it would definitely be a big order. It could be the start of a wonderful business for her."

"So what does this have to do with Papa Pete?" I asked.

"He's working with your mom on the salami samples for tomorrow," Dad said. "They're mixing up some new batches. Papa Pete felt the salami needed more garlic."

I smiled. Papa Pete thinks everything needs

more garlic. He thinks plain garlic needs more garlic.

The light changed, and my dad stepped out into the street.

"This is great news," I whispered to Frankie.

"Why? Because you're going to be rich?"

"No," I said. "Because with all the excitement, they'll forget to ask about my report card."

"And the problem disappears," said Frankie. He waved his hands out in front of him, like he was waving his magic wand.

"Well, it won't exactly disappear. I mean, I'll still have to figure out how to explain my grades to my parents, but at least I'll have the whole weekend to talk to Papa Pete and come up with a strategy." I felt like I wanted to sing and dance. I felt like an elephant had been lifted off my back.

"Zengawii," Frankie said. "It's magic, Zip."

He stuck his hand up in the air, and we high-fived.

I started to skip. My luck had turned, and I had soy salami to thank for it.

CHAPTER 10

As you approach my mom's deli, your mouth starts to water whether you want it to or not. It doesn't matter if you've just eaten a thirty-four-course meal and are so full you feel like your stomach's going to explode; you get hungry all over again.

When you pull that glass door open and step inside, you are in the Kingdom of Smells. Sauerkraut and pickle smells come racing in from one side. Hot pastrami and corned beef pour in from the other. Rare roast beef, salami, and sour green tomatoes circle in from behind. Your nose goes into overdrive. But wait a minute—what's that coming in from the counter? *Oh, no!* Pickled herring in cream sauce with onions. Duck—it's nasty, nasty, nasty!

I have never understood who eats pickled herring. When everything else in The Crunchy

Pickle is so incredibly delicious, why would anyone choose a gray, salty fish with white slime all over it? That stuff should have a store of its own. Wait a minute, I know who eats it. Ms. Adolf probably does. It matches her gray face.

Papa Pete says pickled herring in cream sauce is an acquired taste. I've noticed that grown-ups say that about everything that's truly disgusting, like lima beans, brussels sprouts, beets, green peppers, and movies in French.

The sandwich counter is at the back of the deli, and in the front are the booths where the customers sit. Papa Pete picked out everything in The Crunchy Pickle himself. The booths are this special shade called periwinkle blue, which Papa Pete says he picked because it was the color of my Grandma Jenny's eyes. He's so proud of how nice the deli looks. He always tells me that the booths are genuine leatherette—which is not as expensive as real leather, but not as cheap as plastic. There are always people inside The Crunchy Pickle, because it's such a cheerful place. And the regular food is extra-delicious. I'm not sure my mom's soy lunch meats are such a big draw.

When we came in, Carlos, the best sandwich maker in New York City, was behind the counter. Even though he's only twenty-three years old, he's worked at the deli for as long as I can remember. He started working there when he was still in high school, because his family had just come from Puerto Rico and they needed the money. Carlos and I always talk about baseball, and sometimes after work, we'll go over to the park, and he gives me batting tips. Carlos has a great arm, and he throws a wicked curveball.

Carlos was building a tongue and swiss on rye for Mrs. Wilcox. I've never understood why anyone would eat tongue. Think about it. A tongue has spent its whole life in a cow's mouth, covered in grass. I'm not even going to mention the cud-chewing part.

"Don't forget the extra Russian dressing on the side," Mrs. Wilcox said to Carlos.

"I already put two in the bag for you," Carlos answered. "And I put in extra pickles for Mr. Wilcox. Really crunchy, just the way he likes them."

"*Muchas gracias*, Carlos," said Mrs. Wilcox.

I think she might have winked at him. All the women who come to The Crunchy Pickle love him. He's a pretty good-looking guy, with his shiny black hair and diamond stud earring. He always wears bright red socks, no matter what else he has on. Frankie says he must have a lot of confidence to wear bright red socks, even with shorts.

As he handed Mrs. Wilcox her takeout, Carlos flashed us a big grin. He's always happy to see us.

"Hey, Hankito," he said. "I saved you a black-and-white." He pulled an oversize cookie that's half vanilla frosting, half chocolate off the tray. It's my favorite because there are so many ways to eat it. You can take one bite and get both chocolate and vanilla. You can break it in half, eat all the chocolate and then vanilla. Or you can start on the chocolate, take a rest, and then have some vanilla.

"Frankie, my man," Carlos said. "Here's your oatmeal-raisin." Frankie's mom wants him to eat whole grains, so he's gotten into oatmeal-and-raisin cookies. They're the most healthy-sounding cookies in the display case.

Carlos turned to Ashley. "*Ah, bonita*, I got your favorite, too," he said. Then he gave Ashley a sugar cookie covered with rainbow covered sprinkles. "A beautiful cookie for a beautiful young lady."

"And what do you want, little man?" Carlos asked Robert.

"Actually, I don't eat sugar," said Robert. "It causes tooth decay."

"Is that what happened to that tooth on the side there? Sugar got it?" Carlos asked Robert.

"No, that was an incisor that had to be removed because it was blocking the molar behind it. My dentist says I have an overcrowded mouth."

"You have an overcrowded brain," said Frankie.

We all laughed and spit bits of cookies everywhere. A few of Ashley's sprinkles stuck onto the glass case.

"This is no laughing matter," Robert went on. "If your teeth are too close together, it traps food particles that create plaque, which hardens and causes decay, not to mention gum disease."

"Hey, little man, you shouldn't talk about that stuff. It's gross."

"That's okay, Carlos," Ashley said. "We're used to it. Robert says anything, anywhere, at any time."

We threw our backpacks down on one of the empty tables and sat down to finish our cookies. My father went to his usual corner booth where he keeps a stash of *New York Times* cross-word puzzle books. As Carlos brought him his favorite drink, a cup of hot water with lemon, my mother came out from the back of the store. She was wearing her white headband, which means she's in her cooking mode. She has lots of blond, curly hair, and when she cooks, food splatters in her hair and stays there. Once she had so much chocolate frosting in her hair that she looked like she had brown hair. The head-band keeps her hair clean and blond.

"Hi kids," she said. "How was school?"

"Fine," we all said at once—probably a little too quickly.

"How'd the spelling contest go?" she asked me.

"It was incredible, Mom. Remember the

trouble I had with 'rhythm' last night? I aced that word today."

"Good for you! Anything else interesting happen today?"

"Nope," I answered, barely looking at her. Okay, I admit it, I felt a little guilty not telling her about my report card. But if you think about it, there was really no need for me to feel guilty about my answer. She asked if anything interesting happened, and I said no. I don't happen to find getting a really bad report card interesting, so technically, I wasn't lying.

"So, how's the soy salami coming?" I asked, changing the subject as quickly as I could.

"Papa Pete and I are having an argument over it," she answered. "He doesn't think it has enough flavor. He went to get more garlic."

"I'm so interested to know all about your recipe, Mom," I said.

"Since when?" she asked, giving me a strange look.

"Since . . . uh . . . last Tuesday," I said. "Or maybe it was Wednesday. Yeah, it was Wednesday that I realized that I should know a lot more about what's in the lunch meats you make."

Just then, the deli door swung open and in came Heather Payne and her mother. Heather Payne is the most perfect girl in our grade. Her mother was smiling. Actually, she was beaming. I knew that spelled trouble for me.

"We're here to get a special cookie for my straight-A student," Mrs. Payne said. "Heather got a perfect report card today."

My mother slowly turned her head in my direction. The silence hung in the air like boiled cabbage fumes.

"*Today* is report card day?" she asked, staring at me with eyes that practically burned a hole in my T-shirt. "I guess that little detail must have slipped your mind, Hank."

"Mom, you know that happens," I said. "My mind is slippery."

I gave her that big smile, the one that shows my top and bottom teeth. Frankie calls it The Attitude Grin. She wasn't buying it.

"I think we should continue this conversation in the back room," she said.

"No problem." I tried to sound casual.

"Bring your backpack, Hank."

It occurred to me that I had better bring

my friends, too. I picked up my backpack and motioned for everyone to follow me.

"What are you going to do, Zip?" Frankie whispered.

"I have no idea," I said with a shrug.

The back room is where all the cooking equipment is: big, shiny ovens for baking, long wood counters for slicing, and big bowls for making potato salad and coleslaw. It's the main kitchen, but it's also my mom's laboratory where she makes up new recipes. I noticed that several of her big meat grinders were going, probably mixing up the recipes she and Papa Pete were working on.

No sooner were we in the back room than my mom spun around on her heels and said, "Let's have it."

"By *it*, I assume you mean my *report card*?" I asked, stalling for time.

"Hank, don't play with me."

"Right, okay," I said. "I'm sure it's here in my backpack."

I dropped to my knees and started to empty my book bag as quickly as I could. I dumped everything out on the floor. While I was taking everything out, my Mom walked over to check the machines that were grinding up her mystery meat. She mixed the ingredients up with a spatula and then came back.

Of course I knew where my report card was. I had tucked the big, brown manila envelope deep inside the secret zipper pocket in which I keep my pencils. I made believe that I couldn't find it.

The room was quiet, except for the whirring of the meat grinder churning up the mystery meat and sound of papers rattling as I emptied my book bag.

"Oh, there's my science workbook," I said, stalling for time. "We're learning such interesting things in science. We're almost done with our unit on astronomy. The solar system is so amazing, isn't it, Ashley?"

I motioned for Ashley to talk to my mom to keep her distracted.

"Why, yes, it is, Mrs. Zipzer," Ashley said. "Did you know that they might have discovered another planet no one even knew was there?" I didn't hear the rest of what Ashley was saying, because I was putting my plan in motion.

I pulled the manila envelope with the report card and Ms. Adolf's letter out of the zipper pocket and slipped it to Frankie.

Frankie gave me a look that asked, "What am I supposed to do with this?"

"Get rid of it," I whispered.

I turned to my mom, a look of surprise on my face.

"My report card's not in here," I said, with shock in my voice. "Maybe I dropped it on the sidewalk while we were walking from school. And, you know, pigeons love to swoop down and pick up paper. They shred it with their beaks and use it to build their nests. I saw one do that on Discovery Kids."

"Hank," my mother said, "I'm waiting."

I rummaged around some more in my backpack. Out of the corner of my eye, I saw Frankie turn and hand my report card to Ashley.

"Frankie," I said, "you don't happen to have my report card, do you?"

Frankie held up both his hands to show that they were empty. "Why would I have your report card?"

Ashley took that opportunity to take the report card and pass it off to Robert. Robert took it and looked for someone to pass it off to. But I was out of friends. There was no one left to pass it to. Then Robert did a brilliant thing. Maybe the most brilliant thing he's ever done in his bony little life. He edged over behind my mother and very quietly dropped the entire envelope into the whirring meat grinder. I watched in amazement as my report card disappeared into the beige mixture—all those D's becoming the new ingredients of soy salami.

My mother was losing patience.

"Henry!"

"Mom," I said, "I don't see it anywhere. Honestly, my report card has disappeared before my very eyes."

And I wasn't even lying.

CHAPTER 11

Papa Pete rushed in, carrying a brown grocery bag.

"Well, if it isn't my grandchildren," he said, giving us each a kiss on the top of the head. Papa Pete knows that I'm the only one who's actually related to him, but he calls all of us his grandkids anyway.

"Sorry I couldn't pick you up today, Hankie," he said to me. "I had to come to your mother's rescue."

"Pop, Hank and I were just having an important conversation," my Mom said.

"What is so important that it can't wait until tomorrow?" he asked. "Now is not the time to talk, Randi. Now is the time to grind meat. If we don't get some zing into that paste you're calling a salami, your order from Mr. Gristediano is going to go out the window."

Papa Pete slipped his butcher's apron over his head and began to sharpen his chopping knife.

"Papa Pete, I need to talk to you sometime," I whispered. "It's about my grades."

"We'll talk tomorrow," he whispered back. "No time to talk now," he said in a loud voice, so no one could see we were whispering. "I've got to save your mother from ruining her business."

"Pop, I'm not ruining the business," my mom said to him.

Papa Pete turned off the meat grinder that was chewing up the last of my report card. He took off the bowl, gave it a sniff, and turned up his nose. I tried to get a look inside the bowl. I could see a few chunks of brown manila paper blended in with the beige soy mixture.

"You will if you try to pass off that soy glue in there as salami," Papa Pete said, shoving the bowl to the end of the counter. "It looks terrible, and it tastes like nothing."

"It tastes like soy," my mother said.

"Which tastes like nothing," Papa Pete insisted. "I rest my case."

He reached inside the brown grocery bag and pulled out several long strands of fresh, purple garlic.

"Now, this is the food of the gods," he said. "Garlic. This will make your taste buds stand up and salute."

My mother shook her head. "Pop, that much garlic will overwhelm the taste of the soy," she said.

"Nonsense, Randi," he answered. "Garlic puts hair on your chest. Isn't that right, men?" He looked at Frankie and me and winked.

We laughed. That's what must have happened to Papa Pete, because he has more hair on his chest than a gorilla—on his face, too. He has a mustache that's so big that he calls it his handlebars.

"Let's get to work, Randi," he said. "I'll help you whip up a batch of salami that tastes like something."

"All right, Pop." My mom sighed. I could tell she had given up the fight. When Papa Pete has a plan, it's pretty hard to talk him out of it. "Hank, we'll continue this conversation tomorrow," she said.

That was good enough for me. I had bought myself another day to figure things out.

Papa Pete reached into his pocket and pulled out a twenty-dollar bill. He rolled it up and slipped it into the palm of my hand.

"On the way home, stop in at McKelty's and get yourself and my other grandkids some root-beer floats," he said. "And tell the Chopped Livers I'll bowl tonight, but I'll be a little late. Your mother and I have some high-level delicatessen work to do."

"So you and Mom aren't going to use the stuff in there for Mr. Gristediano's salami?" I asked, pointing to the bowl with my report card in it.

"I wouldn't give that to a dog," said Papa Pete. "The only thing that stuff is good for is to lie at the bottom of the trash Dumpster."

As we left the back room, I gave Frankie and Ashley a big thumbs-up. My report card was going bye-bye into the trash Dumpster. This had worked out better than I could have hoped for.

"Robert, you're a genius," I whispered, slapping him on the back so hard that he almost fell over. He acts like such an adult that sometimes I forget that Robert's just a pencil-neck eight-year-old. I could feel the bones in his back. He really should eat some more mashed potatoes or something.

"I have an IQ of one hundred thirty-seven," Robert said. "Technically, a genius is someone with an IQ of one-hundred forty and above."

"Do you ever lighten up, Robert?" asked Frankie.

"Actually, no," said Robert.

My dad walked us home, and we had the greatest afternoon. We stopped and had root-beer floats at McKelty's Roll 'N Bowl. When we got back to our apartment, Emily wasn't there. She was playing at her friend Jenna's house, so we had the place to ourselves. Frankie and I played video games while Ashley made a rhinestone mouse pad for her mom's birthday. Robert helped my dad with his crossword puzzle. When Robert told him that a "spider relative with two pairs of eyes" was a horseshoe crab, I thought my dad was going to blast right out of his chair. Those thirteen letters put him in such a good mood that he let us watch cartoons on

TV until it was time for everyone to go home for dinner.

My mom was really happy when she got back from work. She was so filled with her salami dreams that she seemed to have forgotten all about my report card. She could hardly wait until the next day. She said she had a feeling Mr. Gristediano was going to give her a big order. If he did, she promised to take us all on a vacation somewhere. She suggested a weekend in Vermont. My dad wanted to go fly-fishing in Canada. I voted for Costa Rica, because I've always wanted to see a real rain forest. Besides, I figured that if they found out about my report card and got really mad, I could hide in the rain forest and live on bananas. Maybe a monkey family would adopt me. Emily said she wasn't going anyplace where there weren't crocodiles. I suggested we leave Emily at home.

We ate tuna melts and chicken noodle soup for dinner.

"So, when will we find out Mr. Gristediano's decision?" I asked.

"Carlos is delivering the trays of salami to

him tomorrow morning," my mom said. "Mr. Gristediano is having all his managers over for a tasting party. If they like it, we should hear right away."

"They have to like it," I said. "I'm sure you and Papa Pete came up with a great recipe."

"Actually," my mom said, "I have a little secret. Don't tell Papa Pete this, but I went back to my first version of soy salami. I thought his had way too much garlic."

I stopped eating.

"You don't mean that original batch of salami," I said. "The one you were making when I was there at about, say, three-thirty-five?"

"Yes," my mom said. "That's the one. That's the winner. I asked Carlos to roll it up and put it in the fridge. He'll slice it tomorrow morning and deliver the platter first thing."

Oh, no. That was the batch of salami with the special ingredient—my report card. I reached for a glass of water and gulped it down all at once.

"Is anything wrong, honey?" my mom asked.

"Wrong?" I asked. "What could possibly be wrong?"

CHAPTER 12

"May I be excused?" I asked, trying to sound calm, which I wasn't.

"Don't you want dessert?" my mom asked. "I made carrot pudding."

"Wow, Mom," I said. "You really know how to use those vegetables. It's hard to say no to carrot pudding, but I've got to run, if you know what I mean." I glanced toward the bathroom. Parents never say no to the bathroom.

"Of course, darling," my mom said.

I shot out of my chair like a rocket and ran down the hall. My socks had no traction on the wood floors, and I went flying like a speed skater right through the bathroom door. I landed on my tush, wedged between the toilet and the tub. I pulled myself up and turned on the cold water in the sink. I had to splash my face with cold water to stop my cheeks from twitching, which they do when I panic.

I needed to think clearly. Too many thoughts were running through my head all at once. *Why hadn't I just told my parents that I got a lousy report card in the first place? Why did Robert have to throw my report card in the meat grinder? What was he thinking? What's wrong with just a regular wastebasket? Would it be against the law for Robert to do a normal thing for once in his life?*

I splashed more water on my face. My cheeks had pretty much stopped twitching, except for the right one, which still moved every now and then.

Lying is hard, I thought. You have to keep everything straight, and that's hard for me normally. Then I had a radical idea. Maybe I should just tell my parents the whole truth—that I'm not cut out for school. That no matter how hard I try, I'm just never going to make it as a student. My mom would be sad, and my dad would be mad, but I'd tell them, "Hey, you got Emily. She's brilliant. I'm wired differently, and my wires are crossed."

Just thinking about that made my cheeks

start twitching all over again. The cold water wasn't helping. I needed a clear head to sort this all out. I slipped out of the bathroom, went to the telephone, and dialed Frankie's number. His dad answered.

"Hello, Dr. Townsend," I said. "This is Hank. May I talk to Frankie?"

"He's just finishing dinner," Dr. Townsend said. "Can he call you back?"

"Normally he could," I said, "but I have an emergency here. Not the kind with an ambulance or anything. It's the kind that could wait, but shouldn't."

"That sounds important, Hank," said Dr. Townsend. "Hold on."

When Frankie got on the phone, I blurted it out: "Emergency meeting. Basement. Now. Pass it on."

I slammed down the phone, ran to my room, and pulled on my shoes. There was something else I needed, but I couldn't remember what it was. It had just been *on* my mind and now it was *under* it. I looked around, hoping it would come to me. *I don't have time for forgetting now*. Then, thank goodness, I saw my sweatshirt hanging on the back of the chair. That was it—my sweatshirt. I knew I wanted to take it, because the basement where our clubhouse is can get cold in November.

"I'm going downstairs to Frankie's," I called to my parents.

"I'll come with you," my mom said.

"You will? No! I mean, why?"

"It's yoga class night," my mom said. Frankie's mom holds her yoga classes in their living room.

"Oh, right."

"We're going to learn a new position. It's called the cobra."

"Sounds dangerous," I said. "Don't bite yourself."

My mom laughed. I thought about what a nice, cheerful person she is and for a minute considered telling her about my grades right then and there. Maybe she'd be really sweet and understanding. Then my dad walked into the room.

"I'm going play Scrabble with Emily," my dad said. "Hank, why don't you join us?"

Right, me play Scrabble—the guy who got

a *D* in spelling would play Scrabble with a girl genius and a crossword-puzzle nut. Sometimes I think my father doesn't have any idea who I am. Any thought I had of telling my parents about my grades went right out the window.

I escaped into the hall and pushed the elevator button. It always takes a while to get up to the tenth floor. When it landed, I pulled the door open and was face to face with our neighbor, Mrs. Fink.

"Why, thank you, Hank." She smiled as she got out, and I noticed with relief that she was wearing her false teeth, which she doesn't always do. "You're growing into such a gentleman."

My mother came into the hall just as Mrs. Fink stepped out of the elevator.

"Hello, Randi," Mrs. Fink said. *Uh-oh.* This was bad timing, because Mrs. Fink's "Hello, Randi" usually turns into a forty-five-minute conversation about what eating spicy food does to her digestion. I had a crisis on my hands, and there was no time now for intestine talk.

"Mom, you don't want to be late for class," I said, pulling her into the elevator. "The cobra is waiting."

As we were riding down to the fourth floor, my mom looked at me funny.

"You seem nervous tonight," she said. "Is anything going on?"

"Nope," I said, not looking her in the eye.

She pointed to a spot on her hand and smiled. "I know you like the back of my hand, buster," she said. "Something's cooking."

Thank goodness the elevator jerked to a stop on Frankie's floor, and I didn't have to answer her. Frankie yanked the door open and was about to say something to me, when he saw my mom. Instead, he just gestured politely to his front door.

"Go right in, Mrs. Z," he said. "There's great karma in there." You can always count on Frankie to be cool in a hot situation.

After my mom was out, he jumped into the elevator with me. I pushed the B button about ten times, as if that would get us to the basement faster.

"Is Ashley coming?" I asked.

"On her way," he said.

Finally, we reached the basement. As we walked out of the elevator, I could tell that someone had just finished doing laundry. It was warm and the air smelled like soapsuds and bleach. We passed the laundry room and went into the storage room that we use as our clubhouse. Ashley was waiting with a chocolate-chip cookie for me and an oatmeal-pecan one for Frankie.

"What's the big emergency?" she asked.

I dropped myself into one of the sofas that line the wall of our clubhouse.

"You're not going to believe this. You know the batch of soy salami that Robert dropped my report card into?"

"Tell me not to think what I'm thinking," said Frankie, "because what I'm thinking is a bad, bad think."

"I can't, Frankie, because I think I'm thinking what you're thinking."

"Will you guys stop thinking and talk to me?" screamed Ashley.

"My mom decided to send her original batch of salami to Mr. Gristediano tomorrow," I said.

"I think I'm starting to think what you're thinking," Ashley said. She twirled her long ponytail around in her fingers, the way she does when she's worried. When she wears pigtails, she twirls both of them, one with each hand.

I took a deep breath and spilled out the whole ugly truth.

"It's bad, guys," I said. "The salami that is being delivered at ten-thirty tomorrow morning is the very same one that has my report card mushed and squished in it."

"Maybe it's not so bad," Ashley said, trying to sound upbeat. "Maybe the paper got ground up into tiny little bitsy bits, and you can't even tell it's in there."

"Ashweena," said Frankie, "there's no way all that paper could get lost in the salami. We're talking a manila envelope, a report card, and a letter written on legal-size paper. I assume it was legal size. It's got to be. When you have so many nasty things to say, you use legal size."

I put my head in my hands.

"I'm sure the whole batch is ruined," I said. "Now my mom will lose the sale. Her hopes and dreams for the future of lunch meats will go right down the drain, and it will be all my fault."

This was a total nightmare. I was single-handedly putting The Crunchy Pickle out of business. And I was still in trouble. Ms. Adolf was going to want to see a signed report card from my parents. Where was that supposed to come from? I'd have to Scotch tape twenty slices of salami together, and even then, you'd have to be really good at reading meat to decipher it.

"I am such a loser," I said, to no one in particular.

Frankie flopped down next to me.

"Snap out of it, Zip," he said. "You're not going to just sit there and let this happen. That's not the Hank Zipzer I know. Breathe, Zip. Let the oxygen flow to promote thinking."

"There's no way out of this," I said. "It's not like we can just find our way over to Mr. Gristediano's apartment—wherever that is— and happen to arrive just as Carlos is delivering the tray and bump into him so the salami goes all over the street and gets eaten by a dog and has to be replaced by a new batch."

"Actually, why not?" came a familiar, uninvited voice from the door.

We whipped around and there he was— Robert.

"When Napoleon invaded Russia, he took the shortest route—through France," said Robert.

"Who is Napoleon?" I snapped.

"He's dead," said Robert. "But when he wasn't, he was a very short French general."

"Great, Robert. What does a short, dead French general have to do with a platter of soy salami that is polluted with my rotten report card?"

"I was just using him as an example of basic military strategy," Robert said. "Napoleon knew that the simplest plans are always the best."

"The boy may have a point," said Frankie, getting up off the couch and starting to pace. "We cut off the delivery. We seize the polluted salami. We destroy it. We replace it with a good batch."

Frankie was excited now.

"Do you really think this could work?" I asked.

"We're going to make it work," Frankie said. "And we'll make it work with style. Don't forget, Zip, we are the Magik 3."

"So?"

"So that means we add our own magic touch

to this plan, to make sure your mom gets the biggest order possible."

"You mean we get to do our magic show?" Ashley asked.

"I think we should pretend we are the entertainment, sent by The Crunchy Pickle to perform feats of magic for the guests as they munch," Frankie said.

"Cool," said Ashley. "I'll do my cherry stem trick."

"Let's hold that for another performance, Ashweena," answered Frankie. "The way I see this performance, we'll cover the salami tray with my cape. True, my cape may smell like salami for a couple months after, but I'm willing to make the sacrifice. Once we're in Mr. Gristediano's apartment, we'll gather everyone around and *Zengawii*! I'll pull off my cape and the salami will appear."

"Then we just sit back and wait for the big order to come in," Ashley said.

"I love it," I said.

Ashley gave Frankie a high five. Even Robert nodded with approval.

"You tell your pal Napoleon that he's got

nothing on me," Frankie said to Robert.

"Actually, I would tell him, but as I already pointed out, he's dead," Robert reminded us.

"It's a brilliant plan," said Ashley. "Don't you think so, Hank?"

I didn't know if it was a brilliant plan or not. But I did know one thing. It was our best shot. It was our *only* shot.

CHAPTER 13

We couldn't leave anything to chance. There was no room for mistakes.

It took us more than an hour to work out all the details. Ashley got some paper and wrote down the whole schedule. This is what it looked like:

FRIDAY NIGHT

9:00 p.m.: Call Papa Pete and ask him to meet us in front of our apartment at 9:45 Saturday.

9:15 p.m.: Ask parents if we can take Cheerio for a walk in the park with Papa Pete the next morning.

9:30 p.m.: Phone one another to make any final arrangements.

SATURDAY MORNING

9:45 a.m.: Meet Papa Pete in front of apartment building. Don't forget Cheerio!

9:46 a.m.: Walk to The Crunchy Pickle. Arrive before ten o'clock and hide outside.

10:00 a.m.: Carlos leaves The Crunchy Pickle for his delivery. Follow him to Mr. Gristediano's apartment.

10:20 a.m.: Carlos arrives at Mr. Gristediano's apartment. Turn Cheerio loose on him.

10:21 a.m.: Cheerio runs into Carlos and starts to chew on his pant leg. Knocks tray out of his hands. Salami spills on ground.

10:22 a.m.: Cheerio eats salami, with help from neighboring dogs.

10:25 a.m.: Carlos goes back to The Crunchy Pickle for a new tray of soy salami, the one that Papa Pete made.

10:27 a.m.: Frankie puts on cape and we turn into Magik 3.

10:30 a.m.: Go up to Mr. Gristediano's apartment and apologize for the late delivery.

10:35 a.m.: Entertain store managers with magic show while Carlos is getting the new tray.

11:00 a.m.: Carlos arrives with tray of all new salami.

11:05 a.m.: Smile at all the guests and make sure they love the salami. Tell them how much their order means to The Crunchy Pickle.

11:10 a.m.: Leave Mr. Gristediano's apartment.

11:25 a.m.: Arrive back at our apartment. Notice strange smell coming from Cheerio (probably gas from salami).

11:26 a.m.: Open windows.

11:30 a.m.: Wait for the phone call placing the order.

11:35 a.m.: Celebrate!

I'm telling you, this was a plan that even Napoleon would have been proud of. Now all we had to do was pull it off.

CHAPTER 14

Papa Pete agreed to meet us in the morning. He was curious to know what all the mystery was about, but I told him I'd fill him in later. He laughed and said he needed a little excitement in his life.

I woke up early, which is something I don't usually do on Saturday mornings. At breakfast, my mom and dad were so nervous, wondering whether or not Mr. Gristediano would like the salami, that they didn't pay much attention to where I said I was going. As long as I was with Papa Pete, they knew I'd be safe. Frankie, Ashley, and Robert had gotten the go-ahead from their parents, too.

I had memorized our timetable. At exactly 9:40, I found Cheerio's leash and went to the closet to get my jacket. It wasn't in the closet.

"Has anyone seen my green jacket?" I hollered.

"How many times have I told you, Hank, you have to keep track of your own things," my father answered from the living room.

Now is not a good time for a lecture, I thought. I started to run around like a crazy person, looking for my jacket. I found it on a chair in the hall, just outside Emily's room. There was only one slight problem—Katherine was sitting on it, sound asleep.

"Emily!" I yelled. "Your lizard is on my jacket."

"Just lift her up," called Emily from her room. "She won't bite."

"I'm not touching that thing," I said. "I'll get warts."

Emily stomped out of her room. "People say that about frogs, not iguanas," she said. "And besides, it's a myth. You don't catch warts from frogs. Warts are caused by a virus."

"Fine," I said. "You and Robert can discuss that in detail sometime. I'm sure he'd find it fascinating. Now could you please just pick up that reptile and get her off my jacket?"

"I can't," said Emily. "I just polished my nails, and they're still wet." Emily has this habit of polishing each of her nails a different color. She thinks it's part of her "look." If that's her look, I think she should look elsewhere.

"Emily," I said. "I'm going to count to three and then tell Mom. One . . . two . . ."

"Okay, you don't have to be so bossy about it," Emily said, lifting Katherine up and putting her on her shoulder.

I put my jacket on fast. I was worried that I was going to be late. Then I grabbed Cheerio and opened the door to leave. I turned to say good-bye to my dad. Suddenly, Katherine, who must have fallen in love with my jacket, jumped off Emily and ran across the living room after me. She grabbed onto my pants and crawled up my leg and onto the jacket, digging her claws into the fabric as if it were her long-lost mother or something. I got scared and yelled so loudly that Mrs. Fink came running out of her apartment into the hall. She was in her big pink bathrobe, and she didn't have her teeth in.

I spun around like a madman, trying to unhitch Katherine from my back. It must have worked, because the next thing I knew, Katherine had jumped to the floor. She looked around for a place to go and saw someplace she liked. Unfortunately, that place was Mrs. Fink. Katherine leapt onto the bottom of her big pink bathrobe and crawled all the way up Mrs. Fink until she stopped about three inches from her face.

"*Heeeeeeeeeeeeeelp!*" Mrs. Fink shrieked in a voice that sounded like a wild hyena I once heard on a National Geographic special.

"*Someone heeeeeeeeeeeeeelp me!*"

My mom was the first one out in the hall.

"Emily!" she screamed when she saw Katherine hanging off Mrs. Fink's chest. "Come out here right now."

"I'm polishing my nails," Emily called back.

"Now!" shouted my father, who had joined the group in the hall.

The doors of the other two apartments on our floor flew open. Little Tyler King stuck his head out from behind his mother. He was wearing his Spider-Man pajamas.

"Mommy! Mommy!" he screamed, when he saw what was going on. "There's a big rat on Mrs. Fink's boobies."

Mr. Park from apartment 10D came out and tried to help. He reached out for Katherine, but when she saw him coming, Katherine whipped out her tongue and waved it in front of him. He jumped back, like any sane person would if they saw that long, ugly tongue.

"Call the police!" cried Mrs. Fink.

"Call the fire department!" called Mr. Park.

"Please be calm, everyone!" said my mother. "Katherine won't hurt you."

By now, Emily had arrived on the scene. "Ohhh, she likes you," Emily said to Mrs. Fink.

"Well, I don't like her!" screamed Mrs. Fink.

"She doesn't go to anyone she doesn't like," Emily said.

Emily came over to Mrs. Fink and slowly reached out for Katherine. But Katherine liked it there on Mrs. Fink's chest, and she refused to go to Emily. She dug her claws into the bathrobe and hung on. It was a pathetic sight. Poor Mrs. Fink was pressed up against the wall, her arms spread out like giant eagle wings. She was too scared to move. The only things she moved were her eyeballs, and they were popping out of her head like something you'd see in a cartoon. She looked down at Katherine and whimpered.

"Nice lizard. Go away now."

Katherine stared at Mrs. Fink with her beady eyes, then suddenly stuck her tongue out. Then Mrs. Fink, for some unknown reason, stuck her tongue out at Katherine. Katherine did it back to her. Mrs. Fink stuck her tongue out again, this time a little farther. Katherine waited a second, then shot her tongue right back at Mrs. Fink.

"Look," Emily whispered to me. "They're communicating. It's like a dance."

"The tongue tango." I moaned. "That's so gross, Emily."

"I think it's sweet," Emily said, "and if you didn't have a brain the size of a pea, you'd think so, too."

"I have to go," I said to Emily. "I'm meeting Papa Pete downstairs, and I can't be late."

"You can't go now," Emily answered, grabbing onto my sleeve to stop me. "Look! They're having a breakthrough."

I couldn't believe what I saw. Katherine stuck out her tongue out and actually licked Mrs. Fink on the cheek. Mrs. Fink touched

Katherine's head with her index finger and smiled, showing her pink gums. I guess that's something that appeals to iguanas, because Katherine's tongue shot out and licked Mrs. Fink again.

"Look, Mommy! They're kissing," said Tyler King. "*Eeewww*, that's so yucky!"

"I think it's the sweetest thing I've ever seen," said Emily. She sounded like she was going to cry.

This was too much for me.

"Check, please," I said.

"Where are you going?" Emily asked.

"Listen, I'd love to stay and get all mushy with you reptiles, but Cheerio and I have important business with Papa Pete." I looked at my watch. "Gotta run!"

I really was late. Katherine's little hallway adventure had cost us ten minutes. I grabbed Cheerio and ran as fast as I could down the stairwell.

CHAPTER 15

I've known Mrs. Fink all my life, and I think she's a nice lady. But watching her and Katherine doing the tongue tango was just more than any guy should ever have to see.

Ashley, Frankie, and Robert had already met up with Papa Pete outside. The four of them were waiting for me under the awning of our building.

"You're late, Zip," Frankie said. "What happened to you?"

"Our iguana fell in love with Mrs. Fink," I answered, knowing that would shut him up, and it did. He just grabbed his stomach and pretended he was going to throw up.

"Let's go," said Ashley. "We're late."

"Excuse me, lady and gentlemen. May I ask what it is we're late for?" asked Papa Pete.

"We have to go to the deli," I told Papa Pete.

"I don't have time to explain now, because we have to get there before Carlos leaves on his delivery run."

"He leaves at ten," said Papa Pete. "That gives us exactly five minutes."

We took off down 78th Street toward Broadway. Cheerio tried to keep up with us. His four short legs moved as fast as they could, but they didn't cover much ground. He looked like he was on one of those treadmills people use at the gym. When we came to our first red light, I picked up Cheerio and tucked him under my arm. We waited. It was the longest red light in the history of electricity.

"Don't look at it," Ashley said. "I swear it makes it stay red longer."

We all turned away. When we looked back, it was still red.

I turned to Frankie in desperation.

"Say your magic words," I begged.

Frankie faced the light, put his hands in the air, and said, "Zengawii." The light changed from red to green.

"I am all-powerful," said Frankie, half believing it.

"Actually," said Robert, "the light is set for a minute and twenty-two seconds depending on traffic flow."

"Shut up, Robert," we all said, as we always do.

We crossed Broadway and ran the last block to The Crunchy Pickle. It was one of those crisp, cool New York mornings, a perfect morning for running. In the summer in New York, you don't feel like running because it's hot and you get all sweaty before you even start. In the winter, it's so cold that when you run and breathe hard, the air stings the inside of your nose. But when you run on a fall morning, boy, it feels just right.

We got to the deli, and I pushed the glass door open. Carlos wasn't there, but Vladimir was working behind the counter, putting toothpicks into cheese squares. Vladimir Olefski is our weekend cook and sandwich man. He's from Russia, and he speaks English with a thick accent. I was scared of Vlady at first, because he never smiles and also he has a lot of reddish-blondish hair growing out of his ears. It's not actually that much hair, but as far as I'm concerned, any hair growing out of your ears is a lot. I remember thinking that Vlady reminded me of a werewolf I saw once on a late-night movie when I slept over at Frankie's. Papa Pete tells me not to look at his ears. He says that when a man can stuff a cabbage like Vlady can stuff a cabbage, what's a little ear hair?

Vlady had his back to us, and he was singing this Russian song he always sings. It is the saddest song you've ever heard. Once I asked Vlady what it was about.

"A man looks for fish in Volga River," he said. "No fish there, so he must eat only snow and stale bread. My family sings this song at parties, and we cry like babies." Those Olefskis must be some really fun party animals.

"Hi, Vlady," I said. "Where's Carlos?"

"He is left," Vlady said.

Oh, no! "How long ago?"

"Many minutes before," Vlady answered in his thick Russian accent.

We had counted on following Carlos. How else could we get to Mr. Gristediano's? We didn't even have his address.

"This is bad," said Ashley. "A real fly in the ointment."

"No flies here," Vlady snapped. "I keep place clean."

"Vlady," said Frankie, saying every syllable very clearly. "Do you know the address where Carlos went?"

"He write on paper," Vlady said, pointing to a pad of paper we keep by the phone to write down deliveries.

Ashley grabbed the pad. The top sheet was blank. Obviously, Carlos had taken Mr. Gristediano's address with him.

"Another fly in the ointment," Ashley muttered.

"Pardon, Missy," Vlady said, his blue eyes squinting at Ashley from under his big red eyebrows. "I say *NO FLIES.*"

Frankie looked at the blank pad.

"Carlos must go through a lot of pencils," he said. "He writes hard. Look, every word leaves an impression on the paper underneath."

That was all I needed to hear.

"Vlady," I said, "can I borrow your pencil?"

He took the pencil from behind his ear and handed it to me. I wiped it off quickly, to make sure it didn't have a loose ear hair on it. Then

I laid it on its side and began rubbing the lead back and forth over the blank piece of paper. The paper turned gray, except the parts on which Carlos's pencil had written the address, which stayed white. As I shaded over the whole page, little by little the address popped out.

"I got it," I yelled, looking at the piece of paper. "Five-forty-one Riverside Drive, apartment 4B."

I ripped the page off the pad.

"Let's jet," I said. I looked around for Papa Pete. He had slid into one of the booths with a cup of coffee. "Come on, Papa Pete. We've got to hurry."

"I just got myself a Danish," he said.

"Can you take it to go?" Frankie asked.

"Is it absolutely necessary?" asked Papa Pete.

"Abso-one-hundred-percent-lutely," said Frankie.

"In that case, I think I can," said Papa Pete. He wrapped the Danish in a napkin and shoved it in his pocket.

"Papa Pete, you are the greatest," I said, dashing to the door and holding it open for him.

"Is someone going to tell me what all this is about?" he asked.

"No time now," I said. "Later."

"Okay, Hankie," said Papa Pete. "The mystery continues."

"Close door," Vlady called after us. "No flies."

I tucked Cheerio under my arm, and we tore out onto the street and headed down toward Riverside Drive. It was about four blocks to Mr. Gristediano's apartment.

"We'll never get there before Carlos does," Frankie said.

"I think we have a chance," I said. I happen to know that Carlos is not the fastest delivery guy in town. He is the nicest and the best dressed, but not the fastest.

"I hope I don't get an asthma attack," said Robert, panting hard.

Ashley turned to him and said, "You don't have time, Robert."

"Oh, right," he said.

It may sound amazing to you, but Papa Pete had no trouble keeping up with us. He's in great shape. He's big, but he's solid muscle.

"It's from the bowling," he always says. "Keeps a man fit." I'm sure that walking up and down the stairs to McKelty's Roll 'N Bowl doesn't hurt, either.

We reached 541 Riverside Drive. It was a fancy building with two carved lions out in front. The doorman was leaning on one of them, picking his teeth with a toothpick. He didn't look friendly.

I walked up to him, but before I could open my mouth, old Robert butt in. "Excuse me, Mr. Riverside," he said.

Frankie whipped around and stared at Robert.

"What do you think you're doing?" he whispered.

"I'm calling the man by his name," said Robert. "It's good manners."

"That's not his name, numbskull," said Frankie. "That's the name of the building embroidered on his coat."

"How was I supposed to know?" asked Robert. "I'm only in third grade."

Right. Now he was in the third grade. When he wants to bore you with the name of every mountain range in Asia, he's a college professor, but when he screws up, he's just a third-grader.

I turned to the doorman.

"Has the delivery from The Crunchy Pickle arrived yet for apartment Four-B?" I asked.

"No."

Just as I had thought. Carlos was late. Do I know my delivery guys or what?

"That's excellent," I said, "because we have a very important matter to discuss with the delivery person who's bringing Mr. Gristediano's platters."

"Good for you," the doorman said, adjusting the toothpick in his mouth. "Who's Mr. Gristediano?"

"He lives in apartment Four-B," I said.

"Says you," he answered.

"No, really," I said. "Take a look."

I reached into my pocket and pulled out the paper from the pad at the deli.

"See," I said, pointing to the address. "It's right there in black and white. Five-forty-one Riverside Drive."

He glanced down at the paper, then back at me.

"Funny," he said. "Looks to me like that

says Four-fifty-one Riverside Drive."

I looked down at the paper and stared at it for a minute. I couldn't believe my eyes. It *did* say 451. I must have flipped the numbers around. How could I have been so stupid? I can't even read three numbers the right way.

The truth is, I flip numbers around a lot. Sometimes I flip letters around too. Most of the time, I don't even know I'm doing it.

I hit my hand on the side of my head, as if I could knock some sense into my stupid brain.

"What is wrong with me?" I asked.

Papa Pete put his hand on mine. He has big hands, and when he touches you, it makes you feel safe.

"What's with the hitting yourself in the head?" he asked.

"I'm the stupidest person in the world," was all I could answer.

"This isn't a tragedy, champ," he said. "You just mixed up a couple of numbers. Worse things could happen."

"You don't understand, Papa Pete, "I said. "Now we'll never catch up to Carlos. In fact, he's probably already delivered the salami platter to Mr. Gristediano."

"So?" asked Papa Pete. "What's wrong with that?"

"Everything. Once Mr. Gristediano tastes that salami, it's over for us."

"What are you talking about?" he asked. "The salami is delicious. I made it myself."

"No." I tried to explain. "You made another batch, not that one. There's something terribly wrong with the salami Carlos is taking to Mr. Gristediano. I ruined it. And now I've ruined Mom's business and her whole future, too. It's all my fault."

I could feel the tears welling up at the corners of my eyes. Papa Pete looked from Frankie to Ashley to Robert, then back to me.

"Does everyone here know what's going on but me?" he asked.

They nodded.

"Then I think we have to talk," said Papa Pete. "It's time for this mystery to end."

CHAPTER 16

We sat down on a bench in Riverside Park. A couple little kids were playing nearby. They held hands and spun around in a circle until they got so dizzy that they fell down on the grass. Then they laughed like maniacs, got up, spun around, and fell down again. I love to hear little kids laugh. They sound like they don't have a problem in the world. I watched them for a minute, wishing I were that little again.

"Now, suppose you tell me exactly what is going on," Papa Pete began.

"I don't know where to start," I said.

"Try the beginning," said Papa Pete.

I took a deep breath. Once I started talking, it felt so good to have the truth all come tumbling out. I told Papa Pete about my report card and the three *D*'s. I explained that I was too ashamed to show that report card to my parents, so I had to pretend to lose it. When I got to the part about the deli and said that we hadn't planned to throw my report card in the meat grinder, Papa Pete held up his hand.

"Are you about to tell me that your report card is ground up in the salami that went to Mr. Gristediano?"

I nodded.

"Actually, there's a letter from Ms. Adolf and a large manila envelope in there, too," Robert added.

"So that's why the big rush to get to Mr. Gristediano's—to get the salami back."

Papa Pete had sure figured it out fast. I wondered if he had ever done anything this bad when he was younger.

"We all feel terrible," Ashley said, "because we were part of this, too."

Papa Pete gathered us around him.

"I want you to listen to me, grandkids," he said. "People are just people. They make mistakes. A guy orders a tuna on rye, and you bring him a roast beef on wheat. It happens."

Papa Pete turned to me.

"But this I know, grandson of mine. You

can't lie to cover up your mistakes. You start with one little lie and it gets bigger and bigger, and before you know it, it's taken over everything. It's like dropping one little piece of herring in a tub of macaroni salad. Before long, the whole tub smells like fish. You follow what I'm saying?"

Actually, he kind of lost me with the herring in the macaroni story, but I think I got the general idea. He was saying that once you tell a lie, you just create more and more trouble for yourself. And boy, was he ever right.

"So we're going to fix this right now," he said. "Hank, you're going to go to Mr. Gristediano's and get the salami back. We don't want anyone to get sick. Then you're going to tell your parents the truth."

In my heart, I knew Papa Pete was right. As much as I didn't want to confess, it had to be done.

Frankie put his hand on my shoulder.

"Zip, buddy, I wish there was a magic word I could say to make this better," he said.

"There is a magic word," said Papa Pete, "and it works every time. It's called *the truth*."

CHAPTER 17

It was two blocks to Mr. Gristediano's apartment, and they seemed like the two longest blocks in the entire city. Now it was Papa Pete who was hurrying, because he was worried that someone would eat one of my *D*'s, which might then cause the Big *D*, that *D* being *diarrhea*. I guess eating paper will do that to you, unless you happen to be a goat.

We tried running up Riverside Drive, but Cheerio was slowing us down again. He was stopping and sniffing every fire hydrant, tree, and doorway along the street. At home, he's happy just to lie on his back and stare at the ceiling, but now, when we were in a hurry, he'd suddenly turned into Mr. Curious.

"Come on, Cheerio, step on it," I said to him.

"Actually, he's checking to see where other dogs have marked their territory," Robert said.

"Robert, let's just say it like it is," said Frankie. "He's sniffing pee."

I picked up Cheerio and tucked him under my arm. He squirmed and wanted to jump out of my grasp, but I gave him no choice in the matter. Papa Pete was in front, running fast. He's pretty light on his feet for a guy who's going to be sixty-eight next June 26.

Here's something I never realized before. Cheerio is heavy when you're running. By the time we reached 451 Riverside Drive, my left arm had fallen asleep. So had Cheerio. I wondered how he could sleep with all that shaking and bouncing going on.

We stopped to catch our breath, which you could actually see coming out of our mouths in little puffs of steam. The building doorman was standing inside, watching us through the fancy glass panes in the door.

"Papa Pete," I said. "Will you tell the doorman he's got to let us in right away?"

"You can do it," he said. "I'll wait downstairs. There's a nice sofa in the lobby."

"You're not coming?"

Papa Pete shook his head. "You know what

you have to do," he said. "This is your mission. Accomplish it."

Papa Pete was right. I had gotten us into this mess, and I had to get us out of it. I marched up to the door, pushed it open, and tried to look very important.

"Sir," I said to the doorman. "We're from The Crunchy Pickle. We have to see Mr. Gristediano on a matter of utmost importance."

"Says who?" the doorman answered, looking me up and down suspiciously. He obviously wasn't too impressed.

"Says all of us," said Frankie, stepping up to my defense. "You know those platters of salami that were delivered a little while ago? We need to take them back immediately. They're very dangerous."

"I never heard of a dangerous salami before," the doorman said. "Except the one my brother-in-law Marvin ate once. Gave him so much gas he nearly blew himself up."

He laughed really loudly.

"Actually, sir, those salamis are filled with pulp," said Robert.

"Yeah," he said, "so was my brother-in-law Marvin." He laughed so hard that the gold buttons on his coat shook. "Hey, I'm just kidding with ya."

"So can we go up now?" Ashley asked, bringing the conversation back around. Ashley's good at getting down to business.

"I'll call and let them know you're coming."

I looked over at Papa Pete on the sofa. He gave me a quick thumbs-up. The doorman rang the button marked 4B.

"Yeah, I got some kids down here from The Crunchy Pickle," he said into the telephone. "They say they got to check on the cold cuts."

He paused and nodded, then turned to us.

"They're expecting you," he said. "Fourth floor. Elevator's on your left."

Before he let us pass, he pointed to Cheerio. "That mutt isn't going to make a mess, is he?"

"Oh, no, sir," I whispered. "He's taking his daily nap, which lasts until at least five this afternoon."

The doorman raised one eyebrow.

"He requires a lot of rest," I said, as we made our way over to the elevator. The lobby was so beautiful, it was a shame no one lived in it. Two sparkly crystal chandeliers dangled from the ceiling. Along the wall to the elevator, there was a mural of people picnicking and dancing in the woods. One of the dancing women was mostly naked, but we were in such a hurry, I didn't even have time to check her out. The elevator was waiting for us and I bolted for it. Ashley and Frankie were right behind me. I pushed 4, and then I noticed we were missing someone.

"Where's Robert?" I said.

Frankie stuck his head out and looked for Robert. There he was, standing in front of the mural, staring at the mostly naked lady.

"Robert! Unpeel your eyeballs and get in here," Frankie said.

Robert turned bright red. "Uh . . . I was just admiring the artwork," he said.

"Right, and my name is Bernice," Frankie answered.

"I just realized something," Frankie said as we rode up. "I forgot my cape."

"No problem," I said, trying to stay calm. "We'll use your jacket."

"No way, Zip. It'll stink of salami, and every

dog in the neighborhood will chase me around for months."

"Okay," I said. "We'll figure something else out."

"That's what I like. We'll go with the flow." Frankie rubbed his hands together and looked me right in the eye. "So what's the plan, man?"

"First," I said, "we'll get to the fourth floor."

"Yeah?"

"Then we'll get out of the elevator."

"Yeah?"

"Then we'll ring the doorbell."

"Good thinking. And then?"

"And then . . ." I stopped and looked at Frankie. He was waiting with great expectation on his face.

"And then I don't have the slightest idea," I said.

CHAPTER 18

The elevator doors opened and we got out. There was only one apartment on the whole floor. I had heard that in some fancy buildings in New York, the apartments are so big that they take up the whole floor of the building. I think it would be cool to live in a place like that. You could skateboard or scooter or Rollerblade up and down the hall and not disturb anyone.

The door to apartment 4B was down at the end of the hall. I glanced at Frankie, Ashley, and Robert. They were expecting me to be a leader. I wasn't going to disappoint them. I shifted Cheerio in my arms and rang the bell, hoping they didn't notice that my finger was shaking all the way to the buzzer.

A tall man in a blue suit answered the door. I don't want to say he was the meanest man I've ever seen, but let's just say he didn't look happy to see us.

"You must be Mr. Gristediano," I said, trying to give him my biggest smile. "I'm Hank Zipzer. Happy to meet you, sir."

I put my hand out in the basic handshake position. Papa Pete says you should always introduce yourself with a hearty handshake. It lets people know you're sincere.

"*Sshhh*," the man said, putting his finger to his lips.

"Of course," I whispered. "Mr. Gristediano, this is very important."

"Mr. Gristediano's over there," the man in the blue suit said. "Can't you see he's conducting an important meeting?"

I stood on my tiptoes and got a peek into the living room. A group of seven or eight people, men and women in dress-up suits, were sitting around on big purple couches. The only man not wearing a tie was standing in front of a long table, on top of which sat my mom's platters. He was holding a cracker with a slice of soy salami on it, and he looked like he was about to put it in his mouth. I had to stop him!

"I have to get in there," I blurted out.

Mr. Blue Suit put his finger to his lips.

"You don't understand," I insisted. "I've got to stop Mr. Gristediano from eating that salami."

"I'm going to have to ask you to leave," he whispered harshly.

"But that salami he's about to eat, it's got my report card in it. Also, a letter from my teacher and a manila envelope. A *large* manila envelope."

Mr. Blue Suit looked at me like I was a number one nutcase and started to close the door in my face. Suddenly, Cheerio woke up. I looked down at him, and he had a look on his face I had never seen before. I could have sworn he was smiling. His nose started to twitch, and his eyes locked on something in the living room.

I followed his gaze to see what had gotten his attention. There, sitting in the middle of the rug listening to Mr. Gristediano, was the largest dog I have ever seen. I think it was a Great Dane. You could have stacked up thirty-five Cheerios and still not have reached its head.

In a split second, Cheerio jumped out of my

arms and made a beeline for that mountain of a dog, which could have easily eaten him for a snack.

"Cheerio!" I yelled. "No!"

Mr. Gristediano stopped talking and turned to look at us. I didn't know what else to do. I waved. My friends were faster at thinking than I was.

Ashley pointed to Mr. Blue Suit's shoes.

"Sir," she said, "your shoe's untied."

As he looked down, the four of us darted around him and ran inside. That Ashley, she has a great mind, even in a crisis.

Cheerio had reached the huge dog and was standing nose to nose with her. Cheerio sniffed her. The Great Dane sniffed back. Her sniff was so powerful that it was like a vacuum cleaner that almost lifted Cheerio's front paws off the ground. Cheerio didn't growl like he usually would have. In fact, it looked like was still smiling.

Could it be? Cheerio was falling in love!

Mr. Gristediano stared at us. "Who are you, and what exactly do you think you're doing?" he demanded. The other people in the room whispered to one another. I couldn't make out their exact words, but I was pretty sure they weren't saying how great it was that we popped in for a visit.

"Mr. Gristediano," I answered, "I can't tell you how happy we are to be here. What a nice house you have."

I had never seen such a fancy apartment. Every space was filled with beautiful objects— African sculptures, china lamps, crystal candlesticks, and even a pink marble chess set.

"You haven't answered my question," Mr. Gristediano said. "*WHO . . . ARE . . . YOU?*"

"Here's the truth, Mr. Gristediano, sir," I said. "It all started yesterday afternoon at about three-twenty, or maybe it was three-twenty-five, when I came into my mom's deli with my report . . ."

Before I had a chance to finish the sentence, I heard a sound coming from Cheerio's throat. It was the weirdest sound he'd ever made, something between a purr and a howling love song.

"I don't like the sound of that, Zip," Frankie whispered. "Your dog's going off the deep end."

Frankie has known Cheerio since he was

a puppy, and he knows that when Cheerio gets started on his spinning thing, there's no stopping him.

Sure enough, Cheerio started to spin. Usually, he chases his tail because he's upset or stressed. I'd never seen him spin happily. He started to spin around so fast that you couldn't tell his head from his tail. I think he was doing it to impress the Great Dane. It worked, because before you know it, Mr. Gristediano's dog got up and started to spin too. She followed Cheerio all around the living room—to the grand piano, around the potted plants, along the front of the fireplace—like two spinning tops completely out of control.

"Nina! Down, girl!" Mr. Gristediano commanded.

"Hank," said Ashley, "I think Cheerio has a crush on Nina."

"He should pick on someone his own size," said Frankie.

But it was too late for that. Cheerio and Nina were spinning around a mile a minute in what I guess was some kind of weird doggie love cha-cha. I'm telling you, those dogs were twirling all across the apartment like two crazed ballerinas.

Now, when Cheerio spins, it can get pretty messy. He's been known to get our rugs twisted up in a bunch or maybe knock over an occasional lamp. But a Great Dane spinning faster than the speed of sound is a whole other thing. Nina was like a tornado traveling across the floor.

"Stop it, Nina! Stop it now!" Mr. Gristediano yelled.

He grabbed her collar. Nina escaped his reach and followed Cheerio, who had twirled himself under the coffee table. Nina tried to get under there, too, but she couldn't fit, so she spun around next to it. *SWISH!* Her tail whipped around and landed smack on the pink chess set. The pieces shot into the air like missiles, and all the well-dressed people sitting on the couch scattered so they wouldn't get hit by a flying bishop or a knight on horseback.

"What on earth is going on?" asked a woman with short, black hair.

"Take cover!" hollered a chubby man with a bow tie. He crawled behind the couch, but he wasn't fast enough to avoid getting smacked in the behind by a flying rook. Luckily, his tush was well padded, and the chess piece just bounced off and fell onto the carpet.

One of the pawns landed on Cheerio's tail, and he let out a little yip. He bolted from under the coffee table and spun himself over toward the picture window that looked out at the Hudson River.

"Cheerio!" I hollered. "Come! Or if not come, then stop!"

Nina went galumphing after Cheerio, who was now dangerously close to one of the African sculptures. It was a sculpture of a man holding a baby up to the sky.

"Oh, no," Frankie said.

But *oh, yes*. Nina's tail thrashed into the wooden sculpture. The sculpture toppled, like a quarterback getting sacked. It landed on the floor with a thud. A few of the guests gasped, but one man, who I recognized as the manager of our local Gristediano's, actually chuckled a little.

"Clean up on aisle five," he said, giving the woman next to him a nudge. The woman next to him didn't even laugh a little.

Mr. Blue Suit ran to the sculpture and tried to stand it up again.

"Here, let me help you," I said.

"Stay away, whoever you are!" he yelled. "You've done all the damage you're going to do!"

That's what he thought.

By now, Cheerio and Nina were doing their dance across the center of the room, taking down everything in their path. *Bam* went a vase with blue flowers all over it. *Rip* went the pillows on the fancy purple couch. *Smash* went the carved crystal candlesticks. *Bam! Pow! Crunch*! went the three china ducks on the end table. Boy, if I had ever seen break dancing, this was it.

Cheerio was having the time of his life. If he had cheeks and they weren't furry, they would have been glowing. Nina was having quite a fun time herself. She didn't seem to care that Mr. Gristediano was shouting every command he knew.

"Stay! Lie Down! Sit! Come! Heel! Up! Down! Off!" he screamed.

Nothing was working. All the people in their

business suits were crouched in the corners of the room and behind the sofa. Mr. Gristediano was running after Nina, and I was running after Cheerio. Those two lovesick dogs couldn't have cared less about us. They totally ignored us, spinning their way to the center of the room near the table of my mom's cold cuts. The vibrations made the platters rattle and shake. One of the platters had shifted to the edge of the table and was about to fall. I pushed it back and grabbed a slice of soy salami from it. I held it up.

"Here, Cheerio!" I said. "A treat!"

I thought if I got his attention, he'd stop spinning for a minute and then I could grab him. Instead, I got Nina's attention, which was not my plan.

Nina jumped up to get the salami, and as she came down, her giant tail swept across the table, knocking all the platters into the air. There were trays of lunch meat sailing around like Frisbees. Slices of soy salami flew everywhere, scattering like fireworks on the Fourth of July. Nina was grabbing them out of the air. She got them before they even hit the ground, ate some of them, and gave a few to Cheerio, since jumping isn't exactly his strong suit.

I looked at some of the salami that landed on the rug. I think I saw the word *sloppy* in one and the word *fail* in another. I know I saw *Ms. Adolf* in another one—the words, not actually her.

Cheerio must have gotten one with a big chunk of something in it, because he was having a tough time chewing up his slice. I looked down at him. He held the salami between his front paws, trying like crazy to gnaw through a chunk of manila folder that was wadded up in it. He was so busy concentrating that he was standing still for the first time since he crashed the party.

"Let's get him," I said to the others.

Frankie, Ashley, Robert, and I joined hands and made a tight circle. We crept up on him, and before he could say "arf," we had him surrounded. I scooped him up and held him tight in my arms.

Poor Cheerio. Love was hard on him. He was exhausted. His little heart was racing, and he was panting. His tongue was hanging out of his mouth, and it still had a piece of soy salami clinging to it. I lifted the salami out of his mouth so he wouldn't choke on it. When I looked at it,

I couldn't believe my eyes. There, lying in the salami for all to see, was my *D* in spelling.

That rotten grade was going to follow me wherever I went.

CHAPTER 19

We're friends, right? So you know me by now—at least a little bit. So you've probably figured out that when bad things happen to me, I make lists in my head.

That's exactly what I did as I looked around the mess that used to Mr. Gristediano's beautiful apartment.

THE NEXT SIX THINGS I PREDICT
WILL HAPPEN TO ME
BY HANK ZIPZER (ALSO KNOWN AS
"CAPTAIN DESTRUCTO")

1. Mr. Gristediano, who is really a genie in disguise, will grant me three wishes. For my first wish, I will wish that none of this ever happened, and it won't have.

2. For my second wish, I will wish for front-row season tickets to the Mets' games. I will get them.

3. While sitting in my box at the Mets game, I will catch more foul balls than any fan ever did.

4. They will offer me a position on the Mets as center fielder. I will accept the position and become the youngest baseball player in America.

5. For my third wish, I will wish for world peace, because that's what Papa Pete always wishes for when he blows out his birthday candles.

6. I will become world famous as a peace-loving baseball star.

CHAPTER 20

You must have guessed by now that Numbers 1 through 6 didn't come true.

Instead, what happened was that Mr. Gristediano called my parents and said that he had to see them right away about a very serious matter.

So much for my predictions. I guess I don't have much future in the crystal ball business.

CHAPTER 21

The hardest thing in the world is waiting, especially when you're waiting for bad news. It only took twenty minutes for my parents to get to Mr. Gristediano's, but it seemed like twenty years.

I asked Papa Pete if he would take Ashley, Frankie, and Robert home. They got into this mess to help me out. I didn't see any reason for them to have to be there to take the blame. Papa Pete told me he was proud of that decision, because I was taking responsibility for my own actions. Before he left, he took my face in his hands and whispered, "Remember, Hankie: *truth*. That's the magic word."

Papa Pete took Cheerio home, too. Poor Cheerio. After Mr. Gristediano's store managers left, Cheerio flopped down next to the fireplace and started to lick the bricks as though they were doggie candy. Don't ask me why. You just can't explain a lot of what Cheerio does. Nina wanted to play with him, but Cheerio had lost all interest in her. That's him. In love one minute, licking bricks the next.

When we were alone, I offered to help Mr. Gristediano clean up the mess in his apartment.

"I think you've done enough damage already," he said. He was holding the pieces of one of the china ducks that had broken in half.

"I bought these ducks in Italy," he said. "I paid a pretty penny for them, as I recall."

"I'm really sorry, Mr. Gristediano," I said. "I didn't mean to break anything."

He didn't answer. I couldn't blame him. I'd be angry at me, too, if I were him.

I bent down and started to pick up the chess pieces that were scattered all across the floor. I had to do something to help. Very carefully, I put them back on the board the way they were supposed to go.

"I see you play chess," Mr. Gristediano said.

"My grandpa taught me."

He began to sweep up the pieces of the blue-flowered vase. It was quiet.

"Do you play chess?" I asked.

"Yes," he said. "My father taught me. He played a lot of chess."

"My dad does crossword puzzles," I said.

"Do you do them, too?"

"No way. I'm a terrible speller."

"Me too," he said. "I was a teenager before I could spell my name correctly."

"Really?"

"Really. Of course, it's not that easy when your name is Vincenzo Giovanni Giuseppe Gristediano. My brother got off easy. His name is Mike."

I laughed. Mr. Gristediano smiled for the first time since the disaster. I couldn't believe he could smile after the all the trouble I had caused.

The doorman downstairs rang the buzzer to say my parents had arrived. I sighed. And there it was—the moment I definitely had not been waiting for.

When my mom came in and saw the mess, she shot me one of her mom looks. It was the one that says, "I don't know what you've done, but how could you have done it?" You've probably gotten that look sometime in your life. My dad had a different look on his face. It was the same one he had the time he went to the dentist for a root canal on his back molar.

"Let me just say that we are so sorry," my mom began.

"Of course, we'll take care of everything that's broken," my dad added.

Mr. Gristediano offered them a seat on the couch. My dad sat down, then reached under his butt and pulled out a piece of salami that had gotten wedged in between the pillows. When he put the salami into the ashtray on the coffee table, I could see a wad of manila envelope mushed up inside it.

"Hank, I think you need to tell your parents what happened here today," Mr. Gristediano said. "I'm sure they would like an explanation, as would I."

Listen, I can make up a story at the drop of a hat, right?

Sitting there on the couch with all of them waiting for me to talk, I was tempted. I could have said that alien worms invaded the salami and planted secret papers in it. I could have said that a superhero named Captain Destructo told me to destroy all lunch meats to save the world from the evils of soy.

Truth, I heard Papa Pete say in my mind's ear.

And so I told the truth, the whole truth, and nothing but the truth.

I started at the very beginning, with the three *D*'s on my report card. I told them how ashamed I was of those grades. I described everything that happened after that—the meat grinder, the recipe switch, the plan to seize the salami. At the end, I even pointed out the chunk of brown manila folder wadded up in the salami on the coffee table.

My parents could not believe what they were hearing. Their mouths were hanging open so wide that you could have planted trees in there.

There are no words to describe how they reacted. Well, maybe there are. *Angry. Embarrassed. Shocked. Disappointed. Hot under the Collar.* (Sorry, that's three words. Oops, I mean four.) If I knew how to spell *infuriated*, I'd put that down too.

I'm out of words now, so let me just say this: Imagine confessing to your mom or dad the worst thing you've ever done. Imagine what their faces would look like. Imagine how their voices would sound. Imagine steam coming out of the top of their heads. You get the picture? Good, because that's just how my parents looked when I finished talking.

"Hank, how could you?" my mom asked. She turned to Mr. Gristediano. "We don't know what Hank was thinking."

"You better get used to your room," my dad said to me, "because you'll be spending all your time there."

"I don't want to butt in to your family business," Mr. Gristediano said, "but may I make a suggestion?"

I was sure he was going to suggest that I go to jail and just eat bread and water.

"This sounds like a situation I had in my own family," Mr. Gristediano said, "with my middle daughter, Angela."

"She ground her report card up into lunch meat, too?" I asked.

"I'm sure she would have liked to," Mr. Gristediano said. "Angela was a very bright child who did very poorly in school. We were always so frustrated with her, and even worse, she was always frustrated with herself. She grew to believe she just wasn't smart."

Boy do I know how she felt, I thought.

"When she got to junior high school, one of Angela's teachers suggested that we get her tested to see if she had any learning differences. It turned out she did. Angela was smart, don't get me wrong. She just learned differently than a lot of other kids do. Do you know that one out of every five kids has learning challenges? I'm sure I had them, too, but when I was growing up, no one even knew there was such a thing."

Mr. Gristediano had trouble learning? No way. He owned the biggest supermarket chain in all of New York.

"Where is Angela now?" my mom asked.

"She's a senior at Columbia University," said Mr. Gristediano. "Once we figured out how she learned best, we got her help and her grades improved dramatically. In fact, everything changed for her."

"I assume you're telling us this for a reason," my dad said.

"As I listened to Hank just now, he reminded

me so much of my Angela, and of myself, too,"
Mr. Gristediano said. "His frustration. His
shame in failing. It's all so unnecessary. I'm no
expert, but if Hank were my son, I'd see about
getting him tested."

I looked over at my mom and dad. We all
said the same thing at the same time: "Mr.
Rock."

That's exactly what Mr. Rock had said after
I spent that week in detention with him. He said
he thought I should be tested to see if I have
learning challenges. He even came over to our
house to tell my parents that. He said exactly
what Mr. Gristediano just said, but without the
Angela part.

When Mr. Rock suggested it, my mom
thought it was a good idea to get me tested, but
my dad refused. Instead, he gave me a lecture
about his Stanley Zipzer theory of success in
school. According to his theory, all you have to
do is "put your butt in your chair and study"
and you'll do fine. End of story.

I've never been able to convince my dad that
I really do study. I study; I just don't learn.

That's not exactly true. I learn some things.

In fact, a lot of things are really easy for me—like memorizing poems or remembering facts from history. My brain just gobbles up that stuff like Hershey's kisses. But other subjects, like spelling or math or drawing—those are really hard. I feel as though when I try to learn those things, my brain says, "Sorry, I'm closed."

Before we left, my parents again offered to pay Mr. Gristediano for everything that Cheerio destroyed.

"I'll tell you what," he said. "You can pay me back by looking into the testing."

My dad didn't say anything, but my mom said she would make arrangements right away.

As we left, I apologized to Mr. Gristediano for causing so much trouble.

"I hope you learned something from everything that happened today," he said. "Growing up is tough, Hank. It's not all smooth sailing." Boy, was he nice.

We were pretty quiet the whole walk home. When we got back to our apartment, my mom went right into her bedroom.

I could hear her dialing the phone.

CHAPTER 22

The testing place looked just like an office at school, which isn't surprising because it was an office at school. The walls were covered with lots of posters that kids had drawn. One showed a colorful butterfly. Another showed a family of puppies in a basket telling whoever was looking at them to read a lot. Those puppies were cute enough to play with.

The tester was Dr. Lynn Berger. She smiled when she talked and kept telling me to take deep breaths and relax. She must have been hanging out with Frankie.

We sat at a round table facing each other. Dr. Berger had a little table right next to her with all her equipment on it: blocks, LEGOS, pictures, pencils, and lots of paper. I mean *lots* of it. Some pages were blank, some had shapes, and some were divided into four squares.

I was nervous. I wasn't sure why. Maybe because I hate taking tests or maybe because I was worried the tests would tell everyone that I was stupid for real.

"Well, shall we begin?" Dr. Berger asked.

"Sure," I answered, not really meaning it.

"Okay. First, I'm going to put a piece of paper in front of you and ask you to draw your family—pets and all."

"Does neatness count?" I asked.

"No, Hank. This is not about you being an artist," Dr. Berger assured me.

I picked up the pencil and stared at the blank piece of white paper for a while. I didn't know how to draw people without making them looking like sticks.

"Can I go get a drink of water?" I asked.

Dr. Berger went to the corner of the room, where there was a water cooler. She pushed the blue button, and water rushed out into a paper cup. She handed me the cup. I took a small sip. I wasn't really thirsty; I had just wanted to get out of there.

"Try to relax, Hank. You're fine," she said.

I drew a little squiggle on the paper. It

looked like a hair.

"Do you understand what I asked for?" Dr. Berger asked. "I want you to draw any kind of picture of your family."

"I understand. I'm sorry," I said. I wasn't exactly positive why I was apologizing, but it sounded right.

I started with Stan the crossword-puzzle man. I tried drawing him sitting at the dining room table doing a crossword puzzle. The table got so big that it took up almost the whole page, so I put the rest of the family there, too. Everyone in the family was on one side of the table, facing me. Mom, Dad, and Emily, with Katherine on her shoulder. I even put a little piece of iguana poop on Emily's sweater. Cheerio was under the table. He came out looking like one of those really long bubbles that I used to blow when I was little.

"I hope this is right," I said to Dr. Berger.

"There are no right or wrong answers on this test," she said.

"I wish all my tests were like that," I said to her.

Dr. Berger laughed, and I started to relax a little bit.

I sat back and looked at my picture. I noticed that we all looked exactly alike—even the iguana. Now I started laughing, because it struck me funny that Mom had three twins, and one of them was a green reptile with a mile-long tongue.

Dr. Berger asked me what was so amusing.

"It's just that my sister's pet iguana looks like her twin," I said.

"Do you all have dinner together?"

"Yes. Every night."

"My, such a lovely family you have."

"That's easy for you to say, because you haven't seen my dad in his boxer shorts."

Wherever that thought came from, please let it go back there right away!

Dr. Berger laughed again. What a great audience.

The next part of the test involved putting a set of odd-shaped blocks into exactly the same pattern as the one drawn on a sheet of paper. Dr. Berger put the blocks in front of me.

I pushed them around until I lined them up perfectly to look just like the pattern on the test paper.

"Wow! You accomplished that task in record time!" Dr. Berger said.

"No kidding. Was I the fastest person ever?"

"I'm sure you are one of them," she said.

That felt good. I began to think that maybe this testing thing was going to work out just fine.

There was reading and vocabulary and listening to numbers and having to repeat them back. I worked puzzles, looked at splattered paintings, and arranged pictures in order. Some of the activities were fun, which made the time really speed by.

When we were all done. Dr. Berger walked me out to the hall, where my parents were waiting. She told us she would go over the results and we would hear back in about a week. Hear what? Hear that I had to change schools? Be left behind? That I'm not smart enough to go to school in the first place?

Boy, seven days can be an awfully long time.

CHAPTER 23

When I'm nervous, my body turns into a fountain. If I'm a little bit nervous, my forehead gets damp. If I'm medium nervous, my palms start to sweat. If I'm really nervous, the armpits get involved. And when I'm scared, my back actually sweats. That may be too much information for you, but there it is, I've said it.

As I sat outside Principal Love's office, all of the above were happening at once. Sweat was trickling out of every part of me that could trickle.

They had been inside there for half an hour—Principal Love, Dr. Berger, and my mom and dad. They said that they wanted to review my test results in private before they called me in. I knew if my tests had turned out normal, my parents would have been out of there in two minutes. I mean, how long does it take to say,

"Great kid you got there"? Not a half an hour, I can tell you that.

Mr. Rock had seen me waiting in the hall. He said he was really glad my parents had agreed to get me tested, and he thought life at PS 87 was going to be much better for me now. Before he left, he handed me a packet of tissues and said I could keep them to mop myself up. It was nice of him not to mention that I was sweating like a hog. After I used the tissues to dry my face, I wadded each one up into a ball and shot them into the wastebasket with my foot. I made seven out of seven, so sitting in the hallway wasn't a total loss.

Frankie came running down the stairs, two at a time.

"How'd you get out of class?" I asked him.

"I volunteered to take the attendance to the office," he said. "Any news from Mole Man?"

"Not yet. I'm pretty nervous."

"Release the tension, Zip," he suggested. "Let it flow up your spine and out your third eye." The third eye is a yoga term for someplace on your body. I have no idea where, but I keep looking for it.

"What kind of freak has three eyes?" asked a big, nasty voice from behind us. That could only be one person. It was Nick McKelty, the last person you want to see when you're waiting to find out if you're normal or not.

"How's the boy genius?" Nick the Tick asked, pointing toward me. "They figure what's wrong with you yet?"

Frankie waved his hands around in the air.

"*Zengawii!*" he said. "That means disappear, McKelty."

"Ms. Adolf sent me to find you," Nick said to Frankie. "She thought you got lost."

"Why would she send *you*?" answered Frankie. "You couldn't find your way out of a paper bag."

"Oh, yeah?" asked McKelty. He scratched his huge, blond head, trying to think of a comeback. "Oh, yeah?" he asked again. Then he turned and left. He's a swift one, that McKelty.

The door opened, and Dr. Berger stepped out.

"Hank, we're ready for you now," she said.

"They're going to tell me I'm stupid," I whispered to Frankie.

"Right, and my name is Bernice," he whispered back.

I took a deep breath and walked into the office.

My mom was holding a yellow pad with her notes on it. My dad had a report in a blue cover. My name was printed on the outside. It was thick—probably twenty pages long. Wow, someone had a lot to say about me.

"We've had a nice chat with your parents," Dr. Berger began. "I want to begin by telling you how much I appreciated your cooperation during the testing process, Hank. You put out your best effort, and I'm proud of you for that."

This wasn't sounding good at all. I've played enough soccer to know that when the coach talks about a good effort, he's usually talking to the losing team.

"We've gone over your test results," Dr. Berger went on. "You have exceptional verbal and reasoning skills, an outstanding vocabulary, great creativity, and a superior intelligence."

"You mean I'm smart?" I asked. I felt all the tension going up my spine and out my third eye.

"Yes, Hank, you are. But along with that . . ."

No, I thought. *Don't say anything more. Just stop right there.*

"The tests also show that you have some learning challenges that have been getting in the way of your school performance," she said.

Well, there it was. I have learning challenges. The truth was out.

I didn't know what to think.

"So what you're saying is that I'm smart and stupid at the same time," I said.

"Absolutely not. You're not stupid at all, Hank," Dr. Berger answered. "Everybody learns in different ways. Our job is to find the best way for you to learn. And I think we can do that."

"How?"

"Oh, there are lots of ways," she said. "We're going to start by working on your study skills so we can help you focus better."

Okay. That didn't sound too bad.

"Sometimes I learn something and then forget it all overnight," I said. "Is that because I don't focus?"

"Perhaps," she said. "We're also going to

talk to your teacher about letting you get information in different ways, like listening to tapes, for example."

I like tapes. This was actually sounding pretty good.

"Listening and watching," I said. "I can do that."

"Good," she answered. "And we'll give you all the time you need to take your tests."

Extra time on tests? Man, I felt like I wanted to jump out of my chair and give Dr. Berger a big kiss on the cheek.

Wait a minute. As I thought more about that, I wasn't sure how I felt about it. I mean, Frankie and Ashley would be finished and at home having dinner, and I'd still be at school, taking a test.

I noticed that my parents had been very quiet during all this.

"Are you mad at me?" I asked them.

"For what?" my mom asked.

"For having learning differences."

My mom reached out and took my hand.

"Of course not, honey. We're going to help you every way we can."

"Good," I said. "How about two real chocolate puddings—not carob—every night for dessert. I think that would help me a lot."

"Same old Hank," my father said. He sounded grumpy, but he was actually smiling.

"We'll all be keeping close track of your progress," said Principal Love.

Uh-oh. That sounded to me like I was going to be putting in extra mole time with Principal Love and the Statue of Liberty there on his face.

"Does that mean I'll be coming to see you more often?" I asked. "Not that I don't enjoy our visits, of course."

"I hope that as your schoolwork improves, we'll see an improvement in your behavior," said Principal Love.

I noticed that I had stopped sweating.

"If you have questions about any of this, don't be afraid to ask," said Dr. Berger. She stood up.

I put out my hand, in the basic handshake position Papa Pete had taught me. She took my hand and shook it.

"Thank you," I said to Dr. Berger. "Thank you for everything."

And you know what? I meant it.

CHAPTER 24

That night we made a homework chart and taped it on the bedroom wall over my desk. On one side, we wrote the name of every subject I study in school. Next to each subject, we made boxes for every night of the week. When I finished my homework in each subject, I would get a sticker in the box.

"That's not fair," said Emily. "I want stickers, too."

The next night, Papa Pete came over with a surprise. He brought two big rolls of stickers. The ones with the snakes on them were for Emily. The ones with the Mets baseballs and Shea Stadium were mine.

"You're going to make it to the World Series of homework," Papa Pete said.

Papa Pete and I went outside on the balcony and sat down. It was cold, but we felt warm with our big jackets on. Papa Pete took out a plastic bag from his pocket. He took out two pickles, our favorite snack. He handed me a garlic dill and took the other one for himself. They were so juicy that they squirted when we bit into them.

"Hankie, let me know if I get any seeds in the old handlebars," he said.

I looked at his mustache. "You're all clear, Papa Pete."

We sat there for a minute, crunching on our pickles and enjoying the air.

"Look at that moon," he said.

If you crane your neck and look around the corner of our balcony, sometimes you can see the moon.

"It's so round. Guess what it reminds me of?" Papa Pete asked.

When most grown-ups ask you to guess at something, they don't really want you to. Papa Pete does.

"Give me a clue," I said.

"It's something you eat."

"A ball of cheddar cheese."

He shook his head no.

"Give me another clue."

"Something your mother makes."

"A matzo ball."

He shook his head no.

"One more clue," I begged.

"Something your mother specializes in."

"A slice of soy salami."

"Bingo," he said.

I was quiet. I still felt really terrible about ruining my mom's chances at that big order for Mr. Gristediano. I hadn't been able to say the words *soy salami* since.

"I really messed up her chances, didn't I?" I asked. "And she was so excited about it, too."

"The good thing about mistakes," said Papa Pete, "is that sometimes we have a chance to make them right."

"I can't fix what I did," I said. "There's no way."

Papa Pete didn't answer. He just sat there and finished his pickle. Then he got to his feet.

"If you were to think of some way," he said, "I happen to be free tomorrow afternoon. You're a smart boy. Think it over."

I thought in the shower. I thought while I

was putting on my pajamas. I thought while I was brushing my teeth. By the time I had put my head on the pillow, I was done thinking. I had thought of a plan.

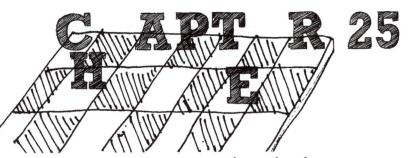

CHAPTER 25

Papa Pete met me after school.

"Where to?" he asked.

"The ninety-nine-cent store," I answered.

The ninety-nine-cent store is on Amsterdam Avenue, right under McKelty's Roll 'N Bowl. I do a lot of my gift shopping there, because ninety-nine cents is just the right price range for my gift budget.

We walked inside, and I went up to the woman at the cash register.

"Excuse me, do you have chess sets?" I asked.

"Aisle thirty-seven," she answered.

You don't get much in the way of a chess set for ninety-nine cents. There were only two choices: a flimsy cardboard one with plastic pieces or a small one that was made for traveling. I liked the small one. It looked like it was made in China, because the faces on the pieces were dragons. I bought the chess set and a silver bow to put on top.

"Where to now?" asked Papa Pete.

"Follow me," I said.

We walked to Riverside Drive. When we reached number 451, the doorman with the shiny gold buttons on his jacket came outside.

"Well, look who's back," he said. "The boy with the exploding salamis." He had himself a good laugh. I couldn't blame him, really.

"Would you please ask Mr. Gristediano if I can come up?" I asked.

"I'll warn him," the doorman said, "so he can put away anything valuable." He laughed again. "Hey, I'm just kidding with ya."

I invited Papa Pete up, but he said that he'd wait downstairs in the park. I walked through the lobby, past the mostly naked lady on the wall. Why is it that both times I'd been there, I didn't have time to stop and admire the artwork, as Robert would say? It wasn't fair.

Mr. Gristediano and Nina were waiting for me at the door. Nina sniffed my clothes. She must have smelled Cheerio, because her tail started to wag like crazy.

"This is for you," I said to Mr. Gristediano, handing him the chess set with the silver bow. "I picked it out myself. It's not much, but I wanted to say thank you for suggesting that I get tested."

"How did that go?" he asked.

"It turns out I do have some learning challenges," I said. I hadn't told anyone that before, but I figured it was time to start. "The woman who tested me says we're going to work on them."

"Good for you," said Mr. Gristediano. "It takes a brave man to be honest with himself."

He looked at the box in his hand. "Should I open this?"

I nodded.

"Why, this is a perfect gift, Hank," he said. "You know how much I like chess. Would you like to come in for a game?"

I was hoping he'd ask.

We sat down at the table by the picture window. I set up the board, and we started to play. It was a nice place for a chess game. When it wasn't your turn, you could look out the window and watch the boats going up and down the Hudson River.

"I skipped lunch today," I said to Mr. Gristediano. "Do you mind if I have a little snack?"

I reached into my backpack and got out the sandwich my mom had made for lunch. I don't think I have to tell you what kind it was. I took a bite.

"What kind of sandwich is it?" Mr. Gristediano asked.

I lifted up the top piece of bread and showed him. "It's soy salami," I said.

I took another bite.

"Mr. Gristediano, do you want to try this? It just might make your taste buds stand up and salute. I can't honestly say it has that effect on me, but it does for a lot of people."

Mr. Gristediano laughed, and I silently thanked Papa Pete for teaching me that expression.

"You're making it sound awfully tempting," he said.

I took the other half of the sandwich and handed it to Mr. Gristediano. He took a bite.

"It's really good for you," I said. "No

preservatives, no artificial colors. I've heard soy salami called the lunch meat of the twenty-first century."

"This is quite good," said Mr. Gristediano. "It wouldn't happen to be from your mother's deli, would it?"

"You mean The Crunchy Pickle at Seventy-seventh and Broadway?" I asked. "The one that's open until six tonight? Why, yes, it is."

I moved my queen across the board.

"By the way, I believe that's checkmate," I said.

I had caught Mr. Gristediano by surprise.

"You're a smart boy, Hank," he said. "I like you."

"Thank you," I said.

He took the last bite of his half of the sandwich.

"And I like your mother's soy salami, too."

CHAPTER 26

"**Guess who came into the deli today!**" my mom said as she rushed into our apartment that night.

"King Kong," said Emily. She and Papa Pete were reading a pop-up book on gorillas.

"Mr. Gristediano!" Mom said. She took off her hat, threw it up in the air, and let out a scream. "He just walked in and said he wanted to place an order."

"How big an order?" my dad asked, looking up from his crossword puzzle.

"One hundred cases!" Mom said.

"That's one thousand nine hundred and twenty salamis!" my father said. He jumped out of his chair, grabbed my mom, and spun her around the room.

Papa Pete flashed me the kind of grin that said we knew something they didn't know.

"Mr. Gristediano said that any woman who can invent the lunch meat of the twenty-first century and raise a fine son like Hank Zipzer deserves to get a great big order!"

"He said that?" I asked.

"Word for word," my mom said. "We have you to thank for this, Hank." She was so happy that she was crying.

My mom gave me such a huge hug that I couldn't catch my breath. Then our whole family started to hug. My dad hugged Emily. Papa Pete hugged my mom. My dad hugged me. Emily hugged Katherine. Cheerio tried to hug himself. I hugged Emily . . . but just for a second. We went hugging crazy, there's no doubt about it.

"Here's to Hank," Papa Pete said.

"Here's to Hank," everyone repeated.

I took a bow.

"You should be very proud of yourself, Son," my dad said.

"Me?" I asked. "What'd I do, Dad?"

"You've brought your grades up—way up."

"I did?"

"Just a few days ago, you had a *D* in salami,"

he said. "And now look. I'm giving you an *A* in salami!"

I threw my arms around my dad and laughed. It was the first *A* my father had given me. Hey, it was my first *A* ever. And it sure felt good.

About the Authors

Henry Winkler is an actor, producer, and director, and he speaks publicly all over the world. In addition, he has a star on Hollywood Boulevard, was presented with the order of the British Empire by the Queen of England, and the jacket he wore as the Fonz hangs in the Smithsonian Museum in Washington, DC. But if you asked him what he was proudest of, he would say, "Writing the Hank Zipzer books with my partner, Lin Oliver." He lives in Los Angeles with his wife, Stacey. They have three children named Jed, Zoe, and Max, and two dogs named Monty and Charlotte. Charlotte catches a ball so well that she could definitely play outfield for the New York Mets.

Lin Oliver is a writer and producer of movies, books, and television series for children and families. She has written more than twenty-five novels for children, and one hundred episodes of television. She is cofounder and executive director of the Society of Children's Book Writers and Illustrators, an international organization of twenty thousand authors and illustrators of children's books. She lives in Los Angeles with her husband, Alan. They have three sons named Theo, Ollie, and Cole. She loves tuna melts, curious kids, any sport that involves a racket, and children's book writers everywhere.